Nick Mama

Winner of the
Bram Stoker Award
Eisner Award

Nominated for the
Shirley Jackson Award
World Fantasy Award
Hugo Award
Locus Award

"How does speculative fiction retain its relevance in an era when daily events feel fictitious and the mere possibility of a future seems speculative? If anyone knows the answer, it's Nick Mamatas."
—Jarett Kobek, author of *I Hate the Internet*

"Mamatas creates a genre that is uniquely him . . . Kerouac's language, Lovecraft's atmosphere, and Bukowski's coarseness."
—*Infinite Text*

"Nick Mamatas is a sharp, sarcastic, amazing writer whose fiction runs the gamut from horror to speculative to literary."
—*Lightspeed*

"Mamatas has drawn upon a wide range of personal and political concerns—the life of the writer, ruminations on parenthood, the fate of left-wing politics—to write stories that are funny, deeply evocative and bewildering."
—*Strange Horizons*

"Mamatas dazzles with a singular, satirical wit."
—Campus Circle

The Planetbreaker's Son

plus

PM PRESS OUTSPOKEN AUTHORS SERIES

PM PRESS OUTSPOKEN AUTHORS SERIES

The Planetbreaker's Son

plus

The Term Paper Artist

plus

Ring, Ring, Ring, Ring, Ring, Ring, Ring

and much more

Nick Mamatas

PM PRESS | 2021

"Ring, Ring, Ring, Ring, Ring, Ring, Ring" was first published in *Transmissions from Punktown*, Dark Regions Press, 2018.

"The Term Paper Artist" was first published in *The Smart Set*, Drexel University, October 2008.

"The Planetbreaker's Son" is original to this volume.

The Planetbreaker's Son
Nick Mamatas © 2021
This edition © PM Press

ISBN (paperback): 978-1-62963-834-8
ISBN (ebook): 978-1-62963-850-8
LCCN: 2020934731

Series editor: Terry Bisson
Cover design by John Yates/www.stealworks.com
Author photograph by author
Insides by Jonathan Rowland

10 9 8 7 6 5 4 3 2 1

Printed in the USA

CONTENTS

The Planetbreaker's Son

1.

It's funny, what survives, and what fades away, when all the world with its many histories is crammed into the tiniest of physical spaces, then smeared across a virtual infinity.

Greek survived. Some of it did. *Ρίχνω μαύρη πέτρα πίσω μου.* "I'm throwing a black stone behind me." Done with a village, done with the port city to which you'd come to make your fortune, done with a life? Pick up a black stone and throw it over your shoulder as you leave, never to return. Take yourself and your stomach full of bitterness, but not a single regret, with you. Everything else you willingly leave behind, or have already lost.

When the planetbreaker's son was young, occasionally his mother would take him outside to see his father at work. It was always on a moonless night, and late. Mother would always wrap him in a blanket too, even during the dog days of summer.

"Well, here it goes," she always said after consulting her watch. It was easy to find the particular planet in the sky—everything is always more obvious on a map—but soon enough Papa would throw a rock over his shoulder and the star would go up, flaring like a newly lit match, then fading to red and black.

Over in realspace, we're all just electrons stored in an object the size of a football field.

At home, where we all live, the sky is just a dome-shaped topological map, screwed on tight over the flat world. The light from a world being broken reached the son's eyes moments after his father tossed the black rock over his shoulder. The planetbreaker would be home soon, or whenever he felt like it.

The planetbreaker didn't like to talk about work. He didn't like it when his son asked questions and didn't listen to the answers, or when he had to repeat himself, or much of anything. The planetbreaker didn't even like the practice of planetbreaking, though he was very good at it.

He did like his son, though he wasn't sure what to do with the boy. The relationship with his wife was over—when the planetbreaker came home, he retired to the couch and caught up on the news. When the air was right, he ventured outside to look for black stones. He helped his son with his homework, watched realspace stories and played realspace games with him on the screens, though games were endlessly frustrating.

It wasn't that the planetbreaker had ever been RS but he had heard about those adventuresome days from his own father. Back when Earth was a thing under one's feet, covered in brown and sometimes green grass, with black and dusty cities, and well-spiced skies that could burn the hair from your nostrils after a hard day's work. RS games were different: for the kid, there were all sorts of little casual exercises in which he saved animals from the wild and got them safely stowed in pointy three-finned rockets.

For the kid to watch Daddy play, there were "mature" games: oh no, an RS meteoroid hit the object and someone has to grow some flesh, learn how to weld, and go outside! Or the object encounters another RS object, and an exchange of personality emulations leads to a political crisis, or an "alien invasion," or a quasi-religious telos—the return to RS, on a new blue Earth, where everyone receives another chance to get it right. Games were dumb, but soothing. Simple decisions, bright colors, and the planetbreaker's son would bark childish advice and smile at his father when the planetbreaker did well.

The planetbreaker and his wife—Zeus and Hera! They fought the way dogs do, all mouth. Father smoldered and snapped, Mother sniped and demeaned him, then Father erupted and Mother squawked in fear and indignation. The walls nearly derezzed, the floor quaked. When Papa rolled his eyes and growled through clenched teeth, the very sky went blank. The little planetbreaker's son loved his mother more than his father, which is right and natural. But he tried, the boy, to amuse his father with jokes about farts and cartoon characters and dancing around. "Are you happy now, Papa?" he asked, often.

"I'm always happy," the planetbreaker said, always, his voice that of a dead man.

The planetbreaker's wife had a much more interesting and vital job than that of her husband. She worked in RS, sliding her being into any number of tentacular waldos to scramble through conduits and down tubes, maintaining and improving the ship. Twice she even engaged in EVA to make repairs to the skin of the football field in which we all live. Not in the flesh, of course, but in a little wheeled repair vehicle that rides along the exterior of the ship on tracks criss-crossing the surface. RS work is nothing like RS fiction—there's no excitement. Should we put a metaphor here? Does it make sense to address the recipient of this message with "RS work is like taping off a room before painting it" or "RS work is the opposite of a spread-sheet in a twenty-first-century office; real things are moved around to represent the virtual." After all, every possible recipient of the message already knows all about RS, our football-field-sized space-craft/ice floe/coffin, and about the post-Singularity virtual habitus (many—the plural of habitus is habitus) in which we experience our disembodied existences.

Ah, but we already said football field at the start! Got us there. Not only is every possible recipient of this message already an inhab-itant of a post-Singularity virtual habitus, but all the actual recipi-ents of the message are well situated within a habitus where "football field" and "spreadsheet" make sense.

So it's easy to imagine—a woman, Caucasian mostly, with straw-colored hair piled on her head and kept in place with bobby pins, takes a seat on a wooden chair and sips tea from a mug. Somewhere in RS, a small machine the size of a waffle iron scuttles from point A to point B, laying atom-thick wiring across the skin of the ship. She goes out with her friends to see a movie, or swim in a pool, or just split a couple bottles of wine, and the magnetic field that scoops up hydrogen from the interstellar medium to fire it out a bank of ramjets astern adjusts ever so slightly. She goes to her job, writing marketing copy for medical devices that she has never seen and that nobody will ever need again, and server loads are calibrated.

The planetbreaker's wife is in a good social position—she knows that she works with RS, that the details of her quotidian life are in fact vitally important to keeping a million tiny stars twinkling in the sky and a spacecraft sucking and shitting its way through space. Not like her husband, who is blind to these things, who sits in his chair and frowns at his son until some inexplicable urge strikes him to visit another world. Not like her son, who thinks RS is all laser swords and telekinetic powers that sandy-haired boys just like him will one day manifest if they're good enough and practice with splayed fingers and pshew-pshew noises.

The planetbreaker's wife wants a second child, but bearing one would cause immense structural damage to the ship. It's the wanting of the second child that keeps the engines grinding forward in RS.

The planetbreaker has always wanted three kids, ever since he himself was a child, though of course he was never actually a child, just some lines of code emulating the desire to become a man and sire three children—boy/girl/TBD. He only has the one boy. One day, when his wife was distracted with her new hobby of zesta-punta and the entirely artificial subsentient lover she had met on the practice cancha, the planetbreaker found his son on the carpet, his thin arms holding open over his head a paperback copy of *Dubliners*.

"Are you really reading that?" the planetbreaker asked his son. "You're seven years old."

"I want to know what it's like to be nine, like the kid in 'Araby.'"

"You should read a Greek story about a nine-year-old, not an Irish one," the planetbreaker said.

"Tell me one," his son said.

"Come with me. We need to find some rocks."

2.

"Is this what RS was like?" the planetbreaker's son asked.

"Sure, sure," said the planetbreaker. "Sure it was." One day, he hopes that his son will realize that "Sure, sure" means "No, but the true answer to your question puts a little pebble in my heart, and I can't bear to tell you directly, but I want you to understand that the answer is no, no, it's always no."

Where planetbreaker and son are right now is only a little bit like RS. There's physics and topology, but everything, everyone, is strangely frictionless. Not a pebble on the sandy red beach, the green sky is not only cloudless but without any change of hue at the horizon, and the purple waves lapping up the shore are always, always, the same size and collapse against the shore at the same rate. A handful of kids—not a filthy knee between them—had swooped by and instantly made friends with the planetbreaker's son. After ten minutes he was leading the crew in some thrilling game of the imagination, with megaexplosions and sudden marriages complete with driftwood babies, then sailing off via cartwheel-spacecraft to realms not yet annihilated. The planetbreaker found a little black pebble on the shore and collected it.

The seaside pension was a nice one. The planetbreaker let his son pull the shrink-wrap off the door—the kid was always excited to tear things apart or knock things over—and take the first exhilarating inhalation of ozone-tinged air.

"Realspace really must be amazing if it's like this," the planetbreaker's son said. He climbed up on one of the twin beds in the spartan room and jumped twice before catching his father's glare and settling down. There was something in the air.

"Is it really so different than being home with your mom?" the planetbreaker asked, changing the subject, he hoped.

"Yeah," said the son. "You're here. I don't get to spend very much time with you." The kid didn't sound sad, or upset, or even wistful necessarily. It was just a statement of fact, and it sounded to the planetbreaker—especially the *spend very much time* construction—like an utterance his son might have picked up from his mother.

"You think fathers and sons spent a lot of time together in real-space?" the planetbreaker asked.

"Yeah!" Then the son reeled off some long and confusing story our planetbreaker didn't understand about a family scrambling to escape icebergs pushing their way down the Thames and board the last spaceship, only for it to be revealed that they'd have to leave their bodies, and the kids all their favorite toys, behind. Maybe it was a Christmas movie of some sort. The toys loomed rather larger in the planetbreaker's son's memory, his father guessed, than in the actual RS story the kid was relaying.

"But there were more and better toys in the now time," the planetbreaker's son concluded. "Can you get me a toy octodog like the one the boy in the RS story had, except it talks and helps me get dressed in the morning?"

The planetbreaker didn't even say sure, sure to that.

"Where do the black rocks come from, Papa?" the planetbreaker's son asked. He couldn't seem to stand silences.

"Didn't you find any at the beach?"

"Not one! And I looked and looked and even when I waded in the water up to my knees it was all sand. Not even any white rocks."

"Does that sound like RS to you?" the planetbreaker said.

"No . . ." the boy said, cautious.

"Yeah," said the planetbreaker. "Do you know something? In this place, the moment you turn off the light after making the decision to get some sleep, you will close your eyes, fall into a pleasant dream, and wake up refreshed in the morning without the slightest problem."

"Really?"

"Try it," said the planetbreaker.

The boy did, with a smile, and with his face all scrunched up as he held his eyes shut as if against a storm.

It took longer than a moment, as the planetbreaker was lying to his son about the properties of the world they were visiting, but the kid fell asleep quickly enough.

This frictionless world's pension had a decent restaurant, which was always open and never crowded, in the same building. The planetbreaker refused to make the decision to sleep and decided to get a midnight snack, maybe observe or interview a couple of the locals.

The planetbreaker wasn't obviously one by the looks of him. Some present themselves as musclebound giants with heads of pure ball lightning spilling forth from the slitted eyeholes of an obsidian facemask, while others take on the seeming of a school of steel-tipped fish burning hot from atmospheric entry. Yet others play Christ Jesus descending from swirling red clouds, or a humble germ that breaks apart the glycoproteins on the lipid bilayer of cell membranes. The planetbreaker was a chubby fellow with curly hair and a thick mustache of the sort that predominated across the Mediterranean and Asia Minor a couple centuries before the Earth died and the survivors abandoned RS. The planetbreaker wasn't necessarily approachable or friendly, but he was human enough to strike up a conversation when he needed to.

He did so now, with a couple filling a two-top next to him. "Hey there," he said. He smiled with his mustache. "You two locals?"

"Sure, sure," said the man. "You're from away?" He seemed intrigued, the man. He had hazel eyes that glimmered as if the small key lights around the restaurant had been deployed just to make that happen. "Welcome, welcome to the Argentum Coast. Name's Jim. This is Pammie," he said, nodding to the woman across from him.

"What brings you by?" Pammie asked. She was another adorable one, with curly hair and the perfect choice of sweater. The pair of them smelled of honeysuckle and musk. The planetbreaker imagined they'd be eating healthy plant-based dishes with perhaps the tenderest of chicken breast for protein.

"Just sampling the algorithms," the planetbreaker said.

"Might you be looking to settle here?" Jim asked. He exchanged a quick, suspicious-seeming glance with Pammie.

There are moments in narratives that carry a weight far more profound than they would in the nonnarrative Thrownness of reality. The look could mean anything: was Jim asking for Pammie's post hoc approval of his utterance? Was "settle" a fraught word given their marital relationship and existence in a world where almost but not all social friction had been excised? All three of them are waiting to order their meals, and there isn't a waitron to be seen, after all. Or were they suspicious of the planetbreaker, which in turn might agitate the man who held the fate of their world in his hands?

The planetbreaker did, in fact, reach for the rock in his pants pocket, but just to adjust it, as a sharp edge was digging into his thigh.

"Do you have kids?" Pammie asked. "I always ask if someone has kids. It's a great conversation-starter, I've found."

"Yes," said the planetbreaker. He was stoic for a long moment, then laughed. "Sure. His name is Yiannis. He's up in the room; fell right asleep after a big day at the beach."

"By himself? Is that safe?" Jim asked.

The planetbreaker shrugged. "He's seven, and the remote control on the entertainment system is locked; the honor bar is barren. If he's by himself he's safe. If someone else were up there with him, that would be trouble." The planetbreaker could be philosophical when it suited his purposes, and his purpose now was taking the measure of this world's locals. He snickered.

Jim glanced over Pammie's shoulder, looking for waitstaff. A bit of grit in the oyster.

"It's perfectly safe," Pammie said. "When I was a child my parents would leave me alone with my brother and sister all the time, and we all grew up fine."

Jim got dark now. "Of course, if you hadn't grown up fine, you wouldn't be here at all. Survivor bias."

"Are you saying that if I didn't grow up to be the person I am, you wouldn't want to be with me?" Pammie took a sip of her water and glared at her seatmate over the rim. "If I was . . . damaged, I wouldn't be worthy of being with you?"

"Should I get the dinner rolls or the breadsticks?" the planetbreaker asked the air between him and the couple.

"If anything had happened, whether damage or something else, you wouldn't be here," Jim said, an edge rising in his voice. "Either you would be someplace else, or you would be someone else. And so would I, wouldn't I?"

"Very philosophical," said the waitress, an older woman who looked much like a bird with her thin limbs and prominent nose and brows. In some worlds, she could have had the body of a humanoid bird, if she so wanted, or if someone else had wanted it. She had appeared just in time, by which we mean a few seconds too late.

The meals were a bit of a distraction, but neither couple quite knew how to excuse themselves from the conversation with the planetbreaker, and the planetbreaker wasn't about to nod and leave them to their chicken breasts.

"Interesting question—I think about it all the time," the planetbreaker said. "I often wonder that about my own child; what if my wife had gotten pregnant a month later, or ten seconds later, from another sperm. He'd be a different child, albeit probably a fairly similar one. His own sibling."

Pammie paled at the mention of sperm. Jim squeezed the handles of his utensils. The planetbreaker felt the temperature rise in the room, heading upward past perfect. He glanced at the kitchen, which would surely be hot, but the double doors were closed.

When he looked back, he saw that the couple were glowing red, like ironlong worked over a fire. They reached for one another across the small, now smoldering table and embraced with viscous limbs. The room began to fall apart, the parquet squares of the floor splitting apart and falling into the infinite black of empty space beneath it.

Planetbreakers! Oh ho, no, just one, just the way a longship of Norsemen viking in straight from Valhalla is a single planetbreaker too. Our planetbreaker flailed and ran, catching a bit of wall here, the roots of an upturned tree there, climbing upward as the world fell to pieces and fluttered into the darkness of null-space. Carpeting, a stainless steel serving tray, in one odd moment a pair of lobsters he used as skates across the void before they disintegrated.

And then came the people—flailing, screaming, some still holding their drinks, or sleeping in their derezzing beds, more than a few holding yogic or qigong positions, some half gone or aflame. The planetbreaker remained whole, swimming against the swirling currents of the disintegrating resort.

The planetbreaker wouldn't have thrown his little black rock over his shoulder, despite the tedium of frictionlessness; the world had been plenty able to accept a little disruption, a bit of rust. His son had liked it!

"Papa!"

There the kid was, clinging to an ottoman like an airline passenger hanging onto sinking wreckage, but he was floating up, or at least farther away from the planetbreaker, who was doing his best to scramble through the ashen confetti of the torn-apart world.

At least the shouting was nearly over, but that just meant the atmosphere was breaking down.

"One sec!"

"Papa, help!"

"Be quiet!" the planetbreaker said. "I'm doing something."

Naturally, we cannot let the planetbreaker's son die, at least not in these early pages. He's the name of the story. And his own father wouldn't let him die, oh no, even if it meant sacrificing himself. Not that it does in this particular case, but the sheer fact of the matter is that our planetbreaker would have tossed his rock over his shoulder right as he walked through his front gate and let his own world vanish if not for the fact that his kid lived there. There wasn't much left of the perfectly frictionless beachworld by the time the planetbreaker managed to swim through the void of floating, flaming ruins and snag his kid's ankle.

He yanked hard, swung the little boy over his head, sending them both spinning, and then let go.

3.

The planetbreaker's parents are retired. They live in the interior of a black hole, where classical physics breaks down, so it is entirely fine if one wishes to move in. The algorithms of the computers running the simulations are fungible, but inside black holes, they just kind of give up and let people do exactly what they want.

But it's very hard to leave once you're in one, so they aren't very popular within our football-field-sized starship zipping through RS.

Kronos and Rhea, those are the grandparents, and they do not leave their home, not ever.

Why did the planetbreaker grab his son by the ankle and fling him toward the black hole to which his parents retired, rather than simply—and it would have been as simple as the blink of an eye—send the poor kid home to his mother? Ah, here comes the little boy now, sailing right past: we're watching from far far away, to avoid being dragged into the black hole ourselves. He's slowing down, slowing, there he goes, red shifting, he's close to the event horizon now, he's probably inside already eating some nice milk and cookies Rhea whipped up, but to us, out here, the planetbreaker's son is frozen on the edge of the event horizon, slowly fading away as nearby photons all get diverted into the black hole and its immense all-crushing gravity.

We know exactly what the planetbreaker's parents are up to, and what his son is up to, even though we are on one side of the event horizon and they exist now on the other side. We can open up the source code from here and see what is happening, read it like a book.

Kronos and Rhea love their little grandson. Kronos hasn't even plucked the boy up and consumed him utterly. Kronos hasn't once contemplated it. That's love, friends! He hadn't swallowed the planetbreaker either, despite the name and provenance, not literally, but Kronos did do something similar: he was one of the many many employees who built the starship. He was no aeronautics engineer or computer scientist or even a sociologist or philosopher; Kronos worked on an assembly line in what was Detroit, manufacturing some of the modules that were launched into space then connected to make the suborbital platform from which robots then constructed the football-field-sized starship full of simulations.

Rhea won a door prize at the defense subcontractor holiday party four years before the ship was completed: right to have her personality and experiences uploaded onto the ship. Kronos was less uploaded and more simply remembered by Rhea, who knew him well enough for the algorithms to fill the rest of him out. He refused to attend subsequent holiday parties and thus missed out on the chance to be fully uploaded—he certainly wasn't worth the energy to do it otherwise. The selector-AIs had made some odd choices, the way lung cancer sometimes strikes down healthy athletes, but for the most part the billion people picked and the eight billion left behind had been so sorted for reasons too obvious to bear.

Kronos tends to repeat himself a lot, about the tyranny of taxes, the μαλακίες in government (there is no government in the black hole, nor is there an anarchy), and whether or not the food is burning. Their son, the planetbreaker, was partially modeled on their true son who had died of leukemia young, partially on the fantasies of his parents, and partially on . . . other things. Incidents and accidents, randomly juxtaposed personality traits, databases about Hellenic populations and the Big Five personality traits, and the child's own cussedness. Also, he was raised in a black hole.

The planetbreaker's son is a happy boy, even when visiting his grandparents in the black hole. He is a little out of sorts now, as he was just thrown from a crumbling planet by his own father, through the endless reaches of notional space, was crushed by hypergravity and smeared against the ring-shaped singularity before being reconstituted by the algorithm into the boy he was. His grandparents smothered him in kisses, Greek-style: first one cheek, then the other, then pinching, hair-mussing, a kiss on the lips, and then two more for the cheeks.

When they were done with him, Rhea cleared the table of tiny coffee cups, and the planetbreaker's son excitedly told his version of the story: there was a beach and these kids and everyone was nice and papa didn't shout so much because everything was easy and happy and then he, the planetbreaker's son himself, got to hang out in a room himself with the TV on any channel he wanted—his mother wasn't even there—and push two beds together to make one big bed to jump on and he touched the ceiling twice with his mega-super jumps like he had always wanted to do at home and then on a third jump he hit the ceiling too but he didn't land on the bed and didn't land on the floor or hurt himself but he fell out of the entire room and then out of the entire building and then came his dad flying up from nowhere like a superhero to catch him and bring him here to visit his grandparents.

"So where is Dad?" he finished up. "I want my mom."

Kronos turned his ancient head to look at Rhea to solve the problem of their grandson. Rhea, the titan of fertility and the earth, produced a wonderful lunch: a Greek salad to start, thick with oil and red tomatoes even a child would relish, cucumbers speckled in rigaini, crumbles of feta salty to even look at; warm pita and chunks of lamb that seemed too rare to be anything but overly chewy but that in the mouth were somehow perfect.

And a little plastic plate of chicken nuggets, microwaved, with ketchup on the side, without a single molecule of the ketchup touching any of the nuggets before the planetbreaker's son had his chance to dip. Fruit punch that had never been anywhere near fruit, not even in the days of RS when there was fruit, and punch, and throats to pour it down, in a little plastic cup. One too small for the planetbreaker's son, but to his grandparents he would always be three years old or so, and not nearly eight.

None of this did anything at all to summon the planetbreaker's mother, of course. Kronos and Rhea don't make calls; they receive them. They don't visit others, they are eager hosts.

"I have to tell you something, Papou," the planetbreaker's son said to Kronos. "You don't have any good RS shows to watch at your house. You should get some. They're fun."

"RS?" Kronos said, rolling his *r* and hissing his *s* so the utterance took nearly ten seconds of subjective time. "RS shows? You don't need no RS shows here, baby. I'll tell you all about RS. RS was very big. Sometimes it was hot, sometimes it rained. I was in an earthquake once, when I was your age. The whole horio—"

"Village," Rhea translated.

"—fell down. Every building crumbled. They loaded every person, every injured person, and goats too, onto the ferry to go to Samos where there was a bigger hospital, but that hospital was full too . . ."

The planetbreaker's son had heard this story before. The hospital in Samos was full of refugees from Syria and their local injured. So it was back onto the ferry, or really another, larger but no more comfortable one capable of the twelve-hour trip through choppy waters to Athens, where the piers were entirely full of ferries from all across the country and one of the city's hospitals had messily collapsed on itself. Finally, some nurses rowed out to the ferry Kronos was on, climbed it like pirates, and started treating the injuries they could. By the time they got to Papou—then a young boy who looked just like the planetbreaker's son in the face, but with black curls for hair—who wasn't that severely hurt, he was tired and dehydrated and a little dizzy from pain, so he vomited right on the nurse's head. Luckily, she was wearing one of those old-fashioned nurse's caps.

The moral of this story is: It's better to live in a black hole, where time has stopped and nothing can escape.

When the planetbreaker's son was born, Kronos and Rhea made the long, to them, journey through the underside of the singularity and out the white hole on the far end of the galaxy, then hopscotched from world to world across the imaginary dome of night, to visit their little agono. The planetbreaker's mother had designed the planet to be a notional northern California town, including the constant threat but never the actualization of major temblors. Kronos lasted three nervous days before retreating to the black hole and taking Rhea with him.

The planetbreaker's son liked the black hole, and loved his grandparents. But he didn't want to be there without either of his parents.

"My mother should come and get me," he said aloud. "Do you think my dad is okay?"

"Oh, he's fine," Rhea told him. "He breaks planets all the time."

"I don't think he broke this one. He found a little rock, but he didn't throw it. He told me I'd get to watch him throw it if he decided to. We were flying through space," said the planetbreaker's son. "He was flying, and I was falling, and he caught me. He looked surprised and scared." The planetbreaker's son started looking surprised, and scared, himself now. Saying it all to his grandparents, and their response of matching bemused expressions, turned his spinal fluid to ice.

Finally, Kronos spoke. "He should not have become a planet-breaker. That is not the son I wanted."

"Oh, it doesn't matter," said Rhea, dismissive. This was an old argument. "He has to do something."

"He could have done something useful with his life! He could live here; we could see the baby all the time," Kronos said. The singularity didn't quite shake or derezz, as it was an arbitrary point of no particular mass or volume or even the energy level of a particular atomic orbital, but something shifted in the scene.

"There are too many worlds," Rhea said, half-explaining it all to the planetbreaker's son. "The RS ship cannot handle all of them, not the way they propagate, with every wish coming true sooner or later."

The planetbreaker's son didn't mind being called a baby, not by his papou. And he especially enjoyed when his yiayia used big words like "propagate," which he almost understood.

"My wish did not come true," said Kronos.

"Oh it did!" said Rhea. "It did!"

"Shouting doesn't make anything better," said the planetbreaker's son. "Do you know that?" His mother asked him that frequently.

"This is your wish, isn't it? We're here with our grandson. It's my wish too," Rhea said. "Why can't you just be happy?"

"My dad shouts a lot too," the planetbreaker's son said.

"I'm happy! I'm happy! I am so happy!" said Kronos. He was a big man, but his voice squeaked like a bird's when he was agitated, and he was agitated now.

"Yeah, you look happy. You make everyone happy. We're all so happy now," Rhea said. "All the happiness in the universe is being drawn in here, and not even love can escape!"

"All I want to do is talk to my grandson and have him grow up to be better than his father!"

"Better than you too!"

"Of course, of course . . ." Kronos said, calming now. "Everyone should be better than me. Everyone is better than me, I know, I know."

The planetbreaker's son said, "Papou, yiayia, you need some good RS shows. You really do. It's okay though; I forgive you." And with that, he left the table. Rhea called after him, while Kronos muttered to himself in Greek about generations of failure and the need for the Theotokos, the very mother of God, to be fucked and sent to hell. The theological implications of a titan making such imprecations were staggering, but in the very depths of a black hole's singularity anything is possible.

4.

Let us not take Rhea too seriously; planetbreaking isn't so much a job that needs to be done as it is an inevitable emergent property of personality emulators and the virtual environments they produce and reproduce. Planets will be broken; people will break them. This does not mean that any particular personality *needs* to be a planetbreaker in order for the system to keep functioning.

Our boy, the son of Kronos and Rhea, isn't even an exceptional planetbreaker. He's neither spectacular nor prolific, and his policies and criteria for throwing that black rock over his shoulder and declaring himself done are as capricious as a Greek god choosing and then abandoning a mortal lover. Where is he now? Not back home, with his spouse who would want explanations and access to her child, or on his way to the swirling dent in space-time where he threw his son as there would be screaming, but on yet another arbitrary world where he could get some work done judging its decorative details.

This planet was a small one, riven by conflicts. There were no more than 120 sentient beings on this world, and most of them had adopted flamboyantly posthuman seemings: genders slipped off like skins from snakes, cigar-smoking bipedal otters, conglomerations of gelatinous blue cubes with pseudopods and orifices forming and dissolving as needed. The only facets of existence the denizens of this little worldoid didn't factionalize over were sartorial-avatarial choices; in his human skin the planetbreaker stood out but was still beneath notice. He was less impressed by this than nonplussed. The planetbreaker stood in the town square and read the embossments; every being on the planet was a public figure, and inclined toward if not skilled at writing manifestos and issuing press releases on myriad topics, though mostly they had to do with the utterances and presumed opinions and mental health issues faced by other citizens. The material was hypertextual and endlessly self-referential across a dozen different senses, some of which the planetbreaker didn't possess, but there were sidenotes and footnotes, albeit incomprehensible ones.

The planetbreaker spent seven wonderful years of subjective time on this world, whose name was in dispute. He joined a faction, then switched sides; he helped create and then cruelly denounced works of both civil architecture and public art, then he worked toward reconsideration and reconciliation. His wife? His son? Time moves differently elsewhere; they'd be fine. The Hellenic theme asserted itself—he was Odysseus, our planetbreaker, now, and Telemachus might be out searching for him and Penelope surely patiently waiting at home and ignoring any potential suitors. Or maybe he'd be back home in the blink of an eye.

Toward the end of his time in this realm, in the sticky afterglow of a social activity halfway between an orgy and a well-choreographed battle royale of masked wrestlers, one of the planetbreaker's lover-opponents dug through the planetbreaker's trousers and found a little black stone.

"This is not part of New Albion's geology," they said, definitively. "It's a coded object."

"It's all coded objects," the planetbreaker said. "We're all coded objects." A murmur went up from the still entwined crowd. Of course they were—are—all coded objects, with no more reality than any other agglomeration of electrons and instructions, but the same could be said of all of RS, no? It comes from qbits, every quark in RS spins according to some rule, and the rules predate the existence of the quarks. It's a primitive wetbrained belief—wetbrained being both a slur that recalls hydroencephaly and a simple reference to the organ everyone on the football-field-sized ship left behind—that everything is particles. Everything is information; everything is a coded object, because the code precedes the objects. There were counterarguments, and they were raised, and some open orifices were offered genitals or pseudopods or extruded nerve ganglia and vice versa, and the being with his rock shot the planetbreaker a sour look for ruining the mood of the room. They were a bit like a praying mantis in an early Edwardian business suit, the shirt unbuttoned to reveal sex organs along the thorax mammalian enough for the planetbreaker to work with.

"Hey, don't blame me," the planetbreaker said. "I'm just a coded object too, coded to say things like 'It's all coded objects.'"

"Take some responsibility for your utterances," the mantis said.

"Funny thing is," the planetbreaker said in a moment of sheer honesty, "that thanks to the coded object you're holding, I don't have to. Or wouldn't have to if I still had it in my hand."

The arguments surrounding him, furious but careful as the mood was festive and clothing items few, subsided.

"Look close," the planetbreaker said.

The mantis did; so did some of the others, untangling themselves to peer. On this planet of faction, unanimity was nearly unheard of save for this one issue:

"You have to leave," said the mantis. A primate of some sort sidled up to them, cupped the rock in the mantis's digits, and said, "I'll hang on to this."

"Why you, Mryon?" demanded another primate.

"I'll hang on to the rock for now," the mantis said, though Mryon the primate did not let go on their forelimb. "But you, sir, must abandon our world now. And without this instrument of genocide."

"You need me," the planetbreaker said. "I . . ."

"We do not need you."

"I don't need you," said one of the others the planetbreaker had engaged with. "I didn't need you and I don't need you. You were fun while you lasted. I'm sure you say that to the worlds, to the coded objects, you erase." She shifted up onto her elbows and rested her chin in her hands.

"I don't," the planetbreaker snapped. "At any rate, would you be happier were I miserable?" He glanced around the room. He was surrounded, naked. The mantis was standing on the pair of trousers they had searched.

"It's a heavy responsibility," said the primate sharing the stone with the mantis. A bit of a struggle was emerging between the two of them. Mryon's grip was strong, and the exoskeletal plates on the mantis's forelimb shifting. The other primate, who had addressed him, had taken up a strategic position on the mantis's other flank, but that could mean anything. Appearances didn't inform alliances here.

"The stone won't work for you," the planetbreaker said.

"It's an object of interest anyway," said Mryon.

"Every breaker is radically different," said the planetbreaker. "Even if you figure out the rock, that won't save you from some other breaker, some other time."

"Like a virus," said the girl with her chin in her hands. "There are ever so many of them, constantly evolving. Just like the old days."

"I wasn't going to do anything. I liked this world. I still like it. I'd like my pants back." The planetbreaker felt much more naked than he actually was, and he was entirely naked. He would have snatched back that rock and tossed it over his shoulder in a second if he could manage it, but the primate was huge, with an orangutan belly and two-meter arms, and the mantislike being now flexing spikes and mandibles.

"I see that you have something to agree on," the planetbreaker said, standing. He thought about covering himself with his hands, but it hardly mattered.

"I doubt we agree about what should be done with you," said the woman, clambering to her feet. "Take me with you? My name's Anna."

"Hello, Anna," the planetbreaker said. "It was nice almost fucking you. Do you own pants?"

"Why would you even want to go with him? You didn't miss much, I promise you," said the mantis.

"Maybe I want to see a planet broken. There are plenty out there that need to go. That's why the stars twinkle, even here, where there are no clouds and it never rains."

"That is not why the stars twinkle!" said the other primate, the one flanking the mantis perhaps in cooperation with Mryon, who still hadn't let go of the rock. Perhaps a generalized brawl would erupt—the orgy had verged on it more than once—and the planetbreaker could snag some clothes and escape.

"Are you saying that there are no defective worlds out there?" Anna said.

"Do you think that traveling with a planetbreaker would be fun and exciting?" demanded the mantis. "That he's a dangerous lad? If he limited himself to extinguishing defective worlds, he'd just be a repairman with a regular route. You get off on mass murder, Anna, admit it!"

"You're the one who penetrated him," Anna reminded the mantis. "And he's obviously a planetbreaker. That's how you knew to rifle through his pants, after pleasuring yourself with him."

"Stars don't twinkle anymore; that's RS business," said the primate. "You're just coded to believe that stars twinkle and so for you they do. Probably far more often and with a more obviously dramatic tempo than stars ever appeared to twinkle back on Earth."

"Not everyone is from Earth!" another orgy participant called out, but the planetbreaker didn't see who it was. He was headed to the door, and a number of beings were following him, arguing among themselves or with Anna, or commenting on the planetbreaker's hairy and acne-covered back, his somehow unusual calves.

A faction of those entities that had no experience of Earth—they were the code-only offspring of uploaded people with RS experience, or personality emulators that emerged from code spontaneously for this or that reason fathomable only to the algorithms of the football-field-sized starship—formed to debate the inherent intersubjectivity of the perception of twinkling stars. In moments, some individuals with RS experience joined the faction, while some emulators betrayed the faction and joined the opposition. A few advocated for both sides simultaneously. Mryon and the mantis were still holding hands.

"May I have the rock back?" the planetbreaker asked them. "It's getting loud in here."

"There's never a reason to harm others," said the mantis. Mryon opened his mouth to disagree, but shut it. He gripped the mantis's forelimb more roughly, and the mantis blinked hard.

"I don't make the rocks. I don't bring them with me. I visit a world and sometimes I find them. As though they've been placed here for me."

"And do you always use a rock when you find it?" asked Mryon.

"No," said the planetbreaker.

"Then it doesn't matter," said the mantis.

"It does matter, because I might step outside right now and just happen to come across another rock, a rock only I can ever find. The worlds give me a lot of chances."

"And many chances to make a good decision instead of a hideous one," said the mantis.

"I agree with that, even when the world doesn't and decides to present me with a quarry of rocks." the planetbreaker said. "I just want some clothes. Keep that particular pebble."

"We could kill you," said Mryon. His voice was low, lower than the planetbreaker should be able to hear over the noise of the ongoing debates and occasional squeal or static burst or great expulsion of gaseous joy, but the planetbreaker felt the threat—nay, the pure factual claim—in the marrow of his bones.

Planetbreakers are not a confederacy; there is no single mission, no flag under which they unite. It's hardly even a vocation at all. It is just a matter of the knack for it, which in truth is fairly evenly distributed across the population, and the circumstances one experiences that lead one to embrace the calling. A mixture of arrogance and ignorance, and just enough intellect and charm to get away with it, helps too. That sometimes entire worlds—most often the uninhabited ones that defy topology and physics (there's a reason Kronos and Rhea live in a black hole) and occasionally those occupied by the worst sorts of beings—do need to be wiped out is a factor as well. Planetbreakers keep the denizens of the football-field-sized starship from the torpor of complacency. They work alone, but:

"There will be others. They might not be a man with a pebble. They might not . . ." the planetbreaker said, smirking now, because he had stopped caring, "sample the local delicacies before making a decision. You can close your portals, keep everyone out, but you'll just end up with native planetbreakers, and they'll break your hearts before cutting a hole in your world and letting all the air out."

"That doesn't mean we shouldn't kill you," Mryon said. "Nobody will come and take revenge on your behalf. The planet will break or it will not, a planetbreaker will come with murder on their mind, or they will not."

"Or they will come and make the only correct choice," said the mantis.

"I'll get him out of here," said Anna, who had collected her own clothes and also a small travel bag. "I promise. We won't come back. He won't come back."

"You're going to make him better with the power of love and compassion?" asked the mantis. If their mandibles allowed them to chuckle, they would have chuckled then. That's why the planet-breaker had liked them so much—no snickering during sex.

"Don't patronize me, ____" Anna said. Whatever the name of the mantis, Anna had the organs to pronounce it within her otherwise human-seeming throat, but the planetbreaker couldn't even comprehend the phonemes with his all-too-human ears.

"Stay," the planetbreaker told Anna. "Or leave. But not with me."

"But—"

"I don't want company. I don't want anything. I just want to go. I was never going to hurt anyone."

"Oh, so we passed your little test, did we?" Now Anna was sore too, testy and moving toward enraged. "Showed you a good time? Convinced you with some argument not to be a raging asshole this once?"

The planetbreaker shrugged. "No, it's not a test. There are no tests, no qualifications for anything, not really. It's just like . . . the weather." It was a weak argument to make, but especially on a world where every argument is honed to a nanoblade edge. But it worked on one level: it was so fatuous that the only rational response was a show of pure contempt. So the planetbreaker got his pants—the other primate who looked like Mryon threw them at him, and Mryon finally snatched the pebble from the hand of the mantis and threw it over his shoulder, albeit to no effect other than a grunt from some fleshy thing still on the floor off which it bounced and spun away, and Anna swigged from her thermos of water and spat two cheeks' worth in the planetbreaker's face just as he pulled his trousers on, and the mantis said, "Have a good life. I mean it."

"Well, it was nice meeting everyone," the planetbreaker said. He wasn't sure whether to put on his pants first or to walk to the door and dress there before leaving, and ultimately tried both at once, slipping on one trouser leg as he limped to the exit.

5.

The planetbreaker's wife took the long trip to a white hole and waited for her son to emerge. The mere fact that she had located a white hole and positioned herself relatively near its ever-spewing event horizon meant that this particular white hole was the one from which her son would emerge, and that he would do so before he fell through the event horizon into the black hole in which his grandparents lived. Kruskal-Szekeres coordinates are amazing, and as they operate only outside the physical singularity, the boy both got to spend a very long time with his grandparents—years, subjectively—and be instantly rescued by his mother at the same moment his father threw him into the black hole.

Now the planetbreaker's wife had two sons, one of whom is a teen, and one the young boy she knew days prior. They occupied the same space, mostly. That is, the teen encompassed the boy, and

100 percent of the boy was held within the coordinates of the teen. The planetbreaker's son and the planetbreaker's son were mutually superimposed upon one another, reticulated, shifting slightly from age to age as their mother's gaze tried to track the different silhouettes of her child.

She said his name, tenderly, and the boy surfaced. Surprised, she said it again, snapping, and out came the teen, overwhelming the image of the boy.

"Well, I don't suppose there is any way to fix this?" she asked her half-grown son.

"Why would you want to fix your own son?" He was as surly as the algorithm knew teens had the reputation of being in the time of the planetbreaker's wife. "Looking for a reset button? Isn't that my father's business?"

The planetbreaker's wife's first impulse was in fact to blame herself—not for any reason in particular, it was just her way to decide that somehow she had failed: to draw clear boundaries with her in-laws, to forbid her husband from taking their son on a planetbreaking expedition, to select the right being to marry in the first place, by stopping with one child despite there being almost no resource issue that could limit family size or composition and perhaps thus encouraging her son to form his own older and younger sibling which the kid had always said he wanted.

"We'll make it work," the planetbreaker's wife said. Of course, she'd blame the planetbreaker for this double state of affairs, as it was his fault. The thought was liberating. If she could find a way to help her son, the credit would go to her, and if not she would still be a good mother. It felt more duplicitous than it was.

The planetbreaker's wife missed her little boy, though he sat next to her on the long voyage home. They took a train, which the kid had always preferred to other modes of travel. Even the teen seemed to like it, though he was awkward in his long limbs, and kept scratching at the scraggly hairs on the underside of his neck.

"Are you feeling all right?" she asked her son. "I'm sure it's disorienting, this new state of being. But are you all right? Is it interesting?" Interesting was a word she hoped would keep her son(s) contemplative and focused on the moment; it sounded distant rather than loving, and she instantly regretted that, but fretting over the ever-shifting blurred dyad in the seat next to her might agitate all three of them even further.

The boy spoke first, and the planetbreaker's wife was relieved. He was always a thoughtful little kid. "It is pretty interesting..." he said, carefully modulating the syllables of that last word: in-ter-est-ing. Then the teen cut in. "I'm going to be like this forever; sharing a body with an eight-year-old. Wait, am I not ever going to grow up either? Am I always going to be"—he screwed up his face, it vanished, it returned—"like this? Sixteen?"

"No fair! He's twice as old as me!" said the boy.

"I am you."

"It's true," said the mother. "You are both you. I would tell you not to argue with yourself, but it's true that people do argue with themselves all the time, isn't it?" She'd hoped the teen would respond, but it was the kid who said, "No, I never argue with myself. That's what people did in the old days."

In the old days, in the days of RS, people didn't just get what they wanted—a train ride, a backyard that was a whole planet, gills or wings. Of course they argued with themselves instead. The planet-breaker's wife had been produced in the starship and her life was entirely virtual, but her job gave her some connection to the real world of meat and particles beyond the interior of the football-field-sized starship. She'd been outside, after a fashion, her personality rolling around on the hull, fixing damage caused by micrometeoroids. It's part of why the train she was on now with her son(s) had such verisimilitude—it's why the planetbreaker's son was so enamored with trains.

"What did they do in the old days about this?" said the teen.

"About what?"

"This, what would you call it, overlay?" said the teen, gesturing at himself as he vanished into the eight-year-old with whom he shared space. The planetbreaker's son, the one his father remembered and threw into the event horizon of a black hole, seemed fairly content. It was only the teen who was agitated. It was the kid's world, after all, and he was sitting next to his mother, whom he loved more than anyone.

"This didn't happen in the old days. It's not actually happening now. I mean, nothing..."

Of course, it was happening. The two children sitting next to her in three-second cycles were as real as she, the planetbreaker's wife, was. And she was real, she knew, because she too had two existences, and one of them was out in RS, outside of the ship. Her decisions out there were utterly material, and thus real.

And it was she, an amaterial being, making them, and thus amateriality was real as well. Further, her amaterial activities were physically possible, the sort of thing she could do were she physical.

The planetbreaker's wife reminded herself of all this fairly frequently, but as her world had fairly rigorous topology and internal consistency—save for her husband leaving for work in order to extinguish a star—her cogitations on the subject of reality were less Existenzphilosophie and more daily pep talk. "You can do it!" with it being things that were actually real—a rare power inside the football-field-sized starship.

"Mommy, just help!" The voice was plaintive, desperate, and half-cracked. The teen. "Do something!"

"Please!" said the child.

The planetbreaker's wife would do something. She had an idea, or the beginnings of one anyway.

"Let's just watch a show for now," she told her son(s). "Can you find something you both agree on?"

They could agree, in broad strokes—right to the RS channel. The teen hadn't seen any more films and shows than the kid had, which was a good sign, the planetbreaker's wife thought, that the teen was a programming glitch rather than the result of real-time experiences on some world. Was a glitch less real than a coded object that had been cultivated in a world matrix with a full suite of experiences?

The planetbreaker's wife figured that she'd soon find out, for better or for worse.

6.

The planetbreaker landed hard on the front lawn of his home on the little world he shared with his wife and son. His home was dark, which was unusual, and the moon new, but somehow the planet-breaker could see dozens of small black pebbles like shards of obsidian glistening between the blades of grass. It was difficult to pick himself up without brushing the side of a finger against one of the planetbreaking stones. He managed to resist the urge to pocket one. This was his world; this was his home.

The planetbreaker let himself in, turned on the lights, and cast around the messy rooms—the kid loved drawing robots and such and had a million toys, his wife was busy with work and rarely picked up, and of course the planetbreaker liked to tell himself that he wasn't good at putting things into order without destroying them—looking for a note. There was none, of course.

The planetbreaker contemplated calling his parents, but that would involve having an extended conversation with them, and making a connection to the interior of a black hole would consume a lot of his world's energy, might even slow down the sky in its revolution around the plane on which his home sat. But surely his wife went to go fetch his son. They'd be back sooner rather than later, and all the planetbreaker would have to do then is fiercely explain why the mission to the frictionless world had gone so wrong, and why he chose to fling his child into the maw of a black hole rather than just sending him home to his mother where he belonged.

Ah yes, and also his extended absence and the side trip to the other world, the one with the orgies and arguments. And there wasn't even a nova in the sky to show that he had just been at work.

There was little else to do but either clean the house, or go back outside and hunt for a rock that felt lucky and true among the many many newly decorating the lawn. Ρίχνω μαύρη πέτρα πίσω μου. It took three minutes of pacing from stoop to lawn and back, then turning on his heel and going back to the lawn, before he finally decided to try to pick up the house.

When the planetbreaker awoke, on the couch he had cleared toys from half, a familiar-looking young man was standing over him, and he shivered in recognition. What was it? The clothes. They belonged to his son, and were suitable for an eight-year-old from the early twenty-first century; some kind of sporty short and a graphic T-shirt with a jive-talking robot from a cartoon that the planetbreaker himself would have watched as a child. But when he had dressed his son the morning of the trip, the robot image had a smile and rounded lines to make it seem juvenile. Now the robot was all angles and bristled with weapons, as in the original anime designed for a more mature audience. Well, an older audience anyway.

The kid's face. It was his face. That of his kid, that of his own dumb self lying on half a couch, his feet tucked awkwardly under his thighs. The planetbreaker's son had always looked like his father, but cuter; Papa's awkward nose and low brow tempered by his wife's pleasant features. The frowning teen looming over him wasn't cute at all; puberty was its typical unkind self, bringing together two appearance algorithms and bidding them to compete for somatic real estate.

"Hi," said this new teen boy, but by the time he said "Dad" and finished the sentence, the planetbreaker's son was the child his father knew again. The planetbreaker's heart soared, and then plummeted. He sat up and over his kid's head he saw his wife standing in the open doorway, then his child changed again and he was looking at a teen's torso and that violent cartoon robot again.

"It's like something out of an RS story," the teenager said. "I mean, a story from the RS times, one of the strange ones." Then the kid asked, "What are those called again? You told me once, Dad."

"Science fiction," said the planetbreaker.

"Is that what you call this?" said the planetbreaker's wife. The utterance had the shape of a question, but it was something else entirely.

7.

Our titular planetbreaker's son was very used to the arguments his parents had—the shouting, the sudden dipping into Greek on the part of his father and his non-Greek mother shouting back, "I don't even understand!" though of course after years of this behavior she does know exactly what his curses and imprecations mean. Her mother-in-law Rhea had carefully translated the stock phrases for her, guffawing and rolling her eyes as she did, years ago. The planetbreaker had learned them from his father, though he never picked up much more Greek than the stuff of rage.

His mother was no slouch either. When the topic wasn't heating up fast enough for her taste, she'd bring out a list of past slights, otherwise forgotten confrontations and sometimes innocuous comments—she'd dig back into their first dates and then say something like, "And I know you're thinking _____" and then insist that her husband defend the vile claims she had manufactured for him.

The teenage planetbreaker's son wasn't quite so used to the shouting as was the boy. Though time in the event horizon of a black hole has no meaning and the kid neither subjectively nor objectively spent six years alone, it had nonetheless been a while for him since. He'd forgotten how to ignore the rage, or rather he'd forgotten that he had to pretend to ignore it for the sake of his parents.

He'd picked up a little rage of his own.

"Will you shut the fuck up?" he bellowed. His mother gasped, his father flew at him, accusing finger pointed, but then it was just the eight-year-old planetbreaker's son looking up at his dad. "Yeah!" said the kid. "It's always too loud and there's too much shouting."

"They're right," said the planetbreaker's wife. "He's right. Our son is right."

"I agree. So please don't start with me. Stop starting with me!" said the planetbreaker.

"What did I even say?"

"I was explaining to our son about science fiction when you butted in . . ." and then the argument started again.

The teen wanted to stay and participate in the fight, to shout at his father when he dominated his mother, to switch sides when Mother's ripostes escalated the situation. In those moments when the kid existed, he strolled casually as he could toward his bedroom and the comfort of his toys, his little books, his endless doodlings of football-field-sized spaceships with incorrect rocket exhaust coming out one end as they dive into black holes or flee from golden space dragons or get torn apart in the space between binary stars. The teenager stayed put in his moments of existence; retreat was cowardice so far as he was concerned. Then one of the parents, the teen didn't even know which, wailed—no words, no sentiments, not even a reaction to anything physical, just primal rage and agony braided together like strands of leather to make a whip—and he stopped staying put and brought his younger self to the bedroom and closed the door.

"Hi," said the little kid to his older self. They were standing before a full-length mirror now.

"Hey, me," said the teen when it was his sliver of time to exist.

"I'm going to be you?"

"Maybe," said the teen. "Who can say? I don't remember this happening to me. I was just you, and me, until a few hours ago."

"So I'm the real one!" The kid smiled at his reflection in the mirror, then the smile, and the kid, vanished just as these words escaped his mouth. "I'm real and you have to go."

"I'm real too," said the teen. "If I'm not real, then who are you talking to?"

"You! Me! Myself!"

"No, you're a crazy kid who needs to be locked up because his parents clearly can't take care of him. Do you want that? And I don't mean being locked up with Yiayia and Papou either—I mean in a little time-out cage somewhere, a real time-out cage with no time in it."

"Will I have toys there?" The kid vanished before he could cry. The frown he wore hinted that tears were to come.

"No," said the teen when he was back.

And the boy cried.

"We need to fix this," said the teen.

"How?" asked the boy. "You can fix it by going away! I go one way, you go another way!"

The teen had to laugh at that. It was crazy kid cartoon logic, not even the stuff of "science fiction," and he understood his own younger self very well indeed. This was a crazy cartoon life, and the kid would never stop demanding that they try to walk in opposite directions. So on the count of three—silent, as the duo knew one another extremely well—they walked, the teen backing up one big step and the kid rushing toward the mirror just as he faded out of the realm of perception of everyone but himself.

A mirror is a method of time travel, or at least transtemporal perception. In RS, light takes time to travel and human minds take time to interpret the information their eyes collect. A reflection is always a bit of old news, if only by the billionth of a second. If one could build a mirror the size of a planet and plop it a light year from one's location, then peer into it with the aid of a sufficiently powerful telescope, one would see in the mirror-planet's reflection a scene from two years prior.

But here aboard the ship, where every being is a bit of code interacting with every object, also bits of code, there is no gap. There is no light traveling from mirror to eye, nor a mirror, nor an eye. The laws of physics are only generally replicated—remember those retirees with their living room in the singularity of a black hole, or the fellow who gets to walk to work though his work takes him to distant-seeming stars?—so when the planetbreaker's son moved in two directions at once, in the mirror, they could see one another, and themselves, overlapped and reticulated, sharing much of the same space.

The boy started to sob for real now, uncontrollably. The only reason his mother didn't storm into the room to comfort him was because he instantly vanished, his cry of "It didn't work!" being swallowed by the reappearance of the teen, who quickly snatched up a small toy drum from the floor, held it up over his head, lifted his leg, and dropped it on his knee right before he disappeared and the kid reappeared. The kid gasped and slapped his hand over his mouth, squeezed his eyes shut. He kicked the drum away, sending it sliding across the carpet and under his little bed. He ran to the door, but the teen reemerged and locked it, albeit from the inside. But now his parents were on the other side, rattling the knob.

"Honey, are you all right?" said the planetbreaker's wife from the other side of the door. "Both of you, that is! Let me in!"

"Let us both in!" said the planetbreaker, his voice sharp. Then calmer, "We're sorry we fought in front of you. I am . . . and your mother is."

"We are. Let us in, sweet boy."

"It's locked," said the sweet boy. "He locked it."

"So unlock it!" said the planetbreaker.

The lock clicked and the door opened. It was the teen.

"We're not real. None of this is real. It's not just me," he said.

The planetbreaker sighed and rolled his eyes, despite telling himself that he shouldn't. There was nothing more tedious than this conversation, so far as he was concerned. Nothing made him throw the black rock over his shoulder faster than coming upon a world where existential skepticism was a major cultural preoccupation. It didn't matter what was real or not; what mattered—

"I should get to live, just like the rest of you. You're no better than me," said the teen. He was replaced by a sniffling child who threw himself at his mother's legs and held on tight.

Well, the planetbreaker thought, that was interesting. He was proud of his boy—of his boy(s)—for embracing the facts of life. It was something he'd always had some trouble with, himself. That was the dumb secret of his planetbreaking. He was avoidant; he wrecked that which held up a mirror to his face, what hinted at responsibility and happiness. What—

The teen was back and hadn't let go of his mother's legs quickly enough. They both tumbled to the floor. The planetbreaker howled, surprised and upset. He grabbed his boy—he had always wanted more than one child and in a way now his wish had come true, and wasn't that the promise made to his parents' generation when they agreed to have their personalities uploaded and launched into space?—and pulled him off his wife, but ended up with his little crying eight-year-old in his arms.

He squeezed the boy tight and kissed him on the left and right side of the kid's salty lips, a proper Greek greeting.

"Put him down!" said his wife, and he startled, almost dropping the boy, then he swallowed a shout when he realized why she was snapping at him. The teen was back as the kid's feet landed on the floor.

"Hmm," said the planetbreaker. Then he glared at his wife and half-grown child, who both had their mouths open, ready to speak or shout and snap or say something he couldn't handle.

"It's me, isn't it?" he said. He held up a hand. "Stop!" The planetbreaker's wife and planetbreaker's son weren't even doing anything. "Just stop, stop and let me speak!"

"We are!" said his wife. "We've stopped!"

"Stop completely! Not a word! Not a glance!" He looked over at his son, still a teen. They waited, the three of them. The planetbreaker's wife clenched her fists, exhaled roughly.

"It is me," said the planetbreaker. "Notice how our kid shifts in time when it's convenient. One or the other can always finish a sentence, whether it's long or short. You know how much I hate interruptions."

"You just hate being interrupted; you don't hate them in general," the planetbreaker's wife said. "And it wasn't convenient when I ended up on the floor."

"But I didn't end up on the floor. The weird thing is that nothing like this has ever happened before," the planetbreaker said. "We've visited my parents any number of times."

"That's just proof that you made it happen this time! You took him with you on your horrible 'job' and then threw him into a black hole!"

The planetbreaker's son, the young one, was back, his eyes wet and forehead wrinkled in a frown.

"Why can't you just be normal?" the planetbreaker's wife demanded. "Why can't you just settle down and play at having a normal job in a normal town with a normal sky?"

"I've always wanted more than one kid, and now I have two," the planetbreaker said, looking at his son. "That's a normal desire, but . . ." He trailed off, shrugged. It was better to be quiet, not to want anything anymore.

"No, you only have me!" said the planetbreaker's son. "And I don't want to be here!" And with that, he wasn't, and the older kid was standing in his place, simmering with identical rage, wearing those now ridiculous seeming-little boy clothes, the beginnings of a mustache sprouting over his lip.

The planetbreaker's son's accent was terrible: "Reehh-no mavree petra piso moo." He ran for the door, his legs long. The planetbreaker thought to tackle him, to fight the kid and bring him down before he did something reckless, insane, but did nothing at all but turn to his wife.

"Stop him!" she demanded.

"How?"

"Will it even work?"

The planetbreaker desperately wanted to say no. His son was no planetbreaker, and even were he one, every planetbreaker was unique. The planetbreaker's son, no matter how surly a teen he was at the moment, could no more delete a world by tossing a rock over his shoulder than our planetbreaker, standing in his living room, powerless and rendered stupid by events both recent and long ago, could delete a planet by melting through the surface and detonating its core.

But, then again, the planetbreaker was getting what he wanted. And like old howling Kronos in his black hole, he wanted a son who would follow in his footsteps.

So he said nothing, which isn't another way of saying no. It's very nearly a way of saying yes.

"Get out there and stop him, now!"

"What do you want me to do, hit him?" the planetbreaker asked. "You're the one who hits him."

The planetbreaker's wife's face fell apart. "Once."

"Three times."

"I was very tired, and angry, and he surprised me. You yell. That's as bad. Don't kid yourself that it's not. I'm sorry I struck him, but you're not sorry for anything you do, not ever."

This was an argument they'd had many times, and the ease with which they slid back into it terrified the planetbreaker. It was easier to fight than to do something to save their child(ren).

"You're right," he said. The planetbreaker's wife didn't acknowledge that. "You're right, okay!" he said, louder. She said something, but the sound of broken glass swallowed her utterance. A black rock landed on the rug between them.

Then the planetbreaker's son's voice, that of the little kid's, floated in too. "Uh-oh. Sorry Mom, sorry Papa. I tried to make sure the big me didn't do it right. Is the house going to be okay? Will my toys disappear?"

"It's fine, honey!" the planetbreaker's wife called out. "Everything is fine!"

"You broke a window! Not everything is fine!" the planetbreaker shouted.

"Relatively speaking, it's fine," said the planetbreaker's wife to her husband. "Your son is a windowbreaker, not a planetbreaker. Let's just do what we can to fix this." She strode past him and walked out the door. The planetbreaker had nothing to do but follow.

As the planetbreaker realized he wanted when he saw it, the teen was back, standing on the lawn, his arms folded across his chest. He didn't know if he could face his kid, his upset little boy, or his wife comforting him. It wasn't as though a teenager was more rational than a child, and if anything a half-grown man could be more rageful, and even violent. He didn't want to have to hit his child. That was the realm of Kronos, eater of the young.

His wife stood a few paces distant from the young man, unsure of herself, possibly even afraid.

"We can try it," said the planetbreaker's wife to her half-grown son.

"But what will it do?" said the teen, testily. It was the sort of snapping that unsuccessfully covers up fear.

"Try what?" asked the planetbreaker.

"It'll determine what's real and what is not," said the planet-breaker's wife. "It's RS."

"Dad!" said the teen. "She wants to sideload me into one of her work machines. That'll kill me! I'm not real! I can't live in RS!"

"That's not the case," said the planetbreaker's wife. She was calm now, constructing an argument as though reading from a manual. She flashed her husband a nervous little smile. "Let's remember that none of this is quite real, but it all makes sense that we want to experience it as real. We're not in real space, and really, we're not actually in real time either. Someone outside of our realm of experience could, for example, read the code and come up with what a sixteen-year-old boy coded-object looks like by closely examining the code responsible for the construction and activities of the eight-year-old boy."

"She wants to put me in one of her RS-machines, cycle me through the system, and see what pops out!"

"Don't call your mother 'she'; she is standing right in front of you," said the planetbreaker.

"Mom wants to kill me!"

"I do not."

The teen flickered out of existence, replaced by the familiar, younger, planetbreaker's son. His mother smiled at him and asked, sweetly, "Would you like to sideload into RS? It'll be like with your dad—he took you to his work, I'll take you to my work. Except my work is completely safe."

The boy said, "No. I know what's going to happen. I'll be a kid forever. I know it. I said so, to me."

"It's not like that—"

"It is; you'll erase me when I'm older and I'll always be a little kid! I want to know what it's like to be nine years old, then ten, then fifteen, and in that order!"

The planetbreaker didn't know if he should even intervene. He smiled to himself. Until recently, his son kept to the usual fantasies kids have of eternal childhood—he'd be an astronaut out in RS, or a planetbreaker, or a soccer coach, married with kids or part of some exciting polycule with various humanoid aliens, but always only himself with his little face and outfits and intense interests in toys and games and dinosaurs, with occasional glances at grown-up literature that was over his head. Now, after a taste of being five-foot something with teen levels of testosterone, the boy actually wanted to grow up, all the way up. That was something, the planetbreaker realized, that he had never managed himself.

"You will, and you already have, baby!" the planetbreaker's wife said. "That's where the Big You comes from. All our trip to RS will do is make sure he comes when he's supposed to, and that you get to stay here with me, and your father, all the time, until you grow up."

"There's a lot of yous, you know," the planetbreaker said to his son. He had no idea if his wife's scheme would work, if going to RS would somehow stop the reticulation of his child, especially since it all seemed to boil down to his, the planetbreaker's, implicit desires, but it was certainly worth a shot and could do no harm. It was best, he thought, to confuse the kid a bit, make him pliable. "Every second you get rewritten; I get rewritten. Your mom does, and the grass does, and the squirrels do." It was like trying to explain to a cat why she needed to get in her carrier and go to the vet. The planetbreaker's son started reticulating quickly again, the boy crying and the teen snarling and spitting, "No way! No way! Half a life is better than none!"

"You'll have your time," said the planetbreaker's wife. "It's inevitable. Flowing through RS in one of the external vehicles is just a way to reset everything..." to the now vague and shouting blur. She was very good at keeping her calm with everyone save her husband, that planetbreaker's wife.

Reset everything, yes, that sounded like a good idea. Such a good idea, in fact, that when the sky turned red and the stars above went black and swole and turned into ten thousand grasping corpora of tentacles bearing down toward his little home to tear it into its component subatomic particles, the planetbreaker almost smiled.

8.

In a moment of simultaneity, the planetbreaker's son(s) screamed and ran to the arms of the planetbreaker's wife. They all fell to their knees and held on tightly to one another. There was no atmospheric disturbance, no shrieking across the sky, no electromagnetic pulse to make the lights flicker or power line transformers explode into a shower of sparks, just the end of the entire world filling the sky and crawling closer.

"Get up," the planetbreaker said as he walked over to his family. "It doesn't matter now if the plan will work or not. There'll be no place to stand in a few minutes, no toys, no house, no zesta-punta."

"Do something, Dad!" said the planetbreaker's son, a child again.

"I did," said the planetbreaker. "That's why they're here. I messed everything up, for a long time. I'm sorry. Mommy will take care of you."

"Yes," said the planetbreaker's wife. She stood up and pulled on her son's wrist, but he was a teen, built to resist, again.

"Stay and fight," said the planetbreaker's half-grown son. Now the wind started picking up, and the boy picked himself up, shaking his hand free from his mother's grip.

"You can stay if you want, but there's no fighting this," said the planetbreaker. "I'd know."

"Why are they even coming? What have we done? What have you done? Do you know that?" The planetbreaker's wife was barking now; there were no tiny children to console or comfort. "What, O Planetbreaker, have you done to rate my planet being broken—because it sure as hell wasn't anything I did!"

The planetbreaker's son was a boy again, and he announced, "Mom said 'hell'!"

"Fucking hell, answer me!"

It was a good question. In truth, the answer was what hadn't the planetbreaker done. Did he fuck around, wander off, extinguish millennia of history between his fingertips the way someone might put out a match? Sure, but in this topsy-turvy world—literally, as the football-field-sized starship corkscrewed its way through space for reasons having to do with maximizing the volume and mass of hydrogen atoms sucked in via the magnetic-field scoops to be fed into the Bussard ramjets—who hadn't? Well, lots of people hadn't, including the planetbreaker's wife, whose sins were relatively few, and their innocent child also did not deserve to suffer except for the algorithmic sins he was born with and which would surely manifest as his programming wound forward in time, past his surly teenage years and into adulthood.

And of course, every planetbreaker had their own reasons for breaking a planet, and only rarely did it make any sense to anyone, not even the 'breakers themselves. They told themselves stories about it afterward.

"Maybe they're responding to the programming glitch," the planetbreaker finally answered.

"We can fix it!"

The planetbreaker's son started crying again. He was the teen again now, and a summertime sky swirling with tentacular death, the special kind of death that is not just an end but an erasure of the beginning and the before, was a bit too much even for him.

"You're not a glitch, baby," the planetbreaker told his son. "But you should get inside with your mother."

"We'll do something fun—make cookies!" said the planetbreaker's wife.

The teen took his mother's proffered hand and together they dashed back inside, practically giggling. Now the lights flickered, and not just the warm lights of home spilling out the windows and on to the lawn, but the very notion of light, the code that created such things as light and shadow.

Time, that old devil, is relative. The planetbreaker's wife and son, now in the house, in the kitchen, are running on a slightly different timeline than the man they left outside on the lawn, and that is a good thing for them. The timeline resets as the kitchen redraws itself when coded agents enter it. Thankfully, the last person in the room had drawn the curtains.

So the two of them can get their bowls, and butter, and eggs, and flour, and start preparing cookies. This is one of the many ways the planetbreaker's wife has of interacting with RS, of sideloading herself into one of the machines stored on the skin of the football-field-sized starship corkscrewing its way through space. Eventually, something will happen outside, and the window code will register a crack, and that crack will be made manifest in the kitchen-object as well as outside, and then time between the two locations will synchronize, but for now—put that in quotes, "now"—the planetbreaker's wife and son have plenty of time to make cookies.

The planetbreaker's wife's every movement influences the machines crawling around on the surface of the ship in RS; the planetbreaker's son oscillates between ages haphazardly, but he helps as he can. The cookies baked quickly, and were still blazing hot when the planetbreaker's wife took a gooey one from the cooling rack, pulled it apart, and offered half to her child. It was the teen who ate it, and she ate her piece as well, and then they were both in RS.

Imagine being the gasoline poured into your car's fuel tank, while also being the extremely competent driver turning the ignition, taking the vehicle out of neutral, and depressing the accelerator. You'd feel everything both ways: the twist of the key and the rush of electrical current in combustion chambers that just made some of you explode. The wheel in your hands, and the slosh of your very self within the vehicle you bid turn. You would be an extremely excellent driver, if you were also the gasoline.

You would not, however, as the planetbreaker's son soon discovered, have a particular age, or gender. The planetbreaker's son feels just like the metal crab performing routine maintenance on the hull of the football-field-sized starship that he, that it, is. The crab is also still the planetbreaker's son; rather than an oscillating reticulation of two similar but not identical identities, the planetbreaker's son is 100 percent virtual boy and 100 percent material crab—two natures in one. We're sure that sounds familiar to you, somehow. And the planetbreaker's wife? Same thing, but she's very used to it. She's in and is a device of her own, one with wheels on rails. Her crabson scuttles after her, experiencing three dimensions and a very different type of time, for the first time ever. The stars scattered across the mostly empty universe are amazing, and the bright stars and the endless void not nearly as cold as you might guess, given that the ship of course radiates significant heat and deep space is an excellent insulator.

The planetbreaker's son isn't reticulated, he isn't a pair of himself, anymore. He is neither eight nor sixteen; he isn't forty or ninety either. He doesn't even feel much like the planetbreaker's son in particular anymore, though he's been toggled to boy for so much longer than any age-moment that some traces of boyness and sonness remain. Offspringness is a binary category and he is still the planetbreaker's child, and then he recalls that he and his mother left his father home, to face down a sky roiling with flaming tentacles. He caught up with his mother—it was easy, he was a freewalking device and not dependent on the veinlike rails on the skin of the ship his mother's vehicle used—and tapped the planetbreaker's wife on the most shoulderlike element of her design. It was a human enough gesture to stop her in her tracks.

9.

And the planetbreaker, buffeted about by an atmospheric phenomenon he didn't create and could not control, hit the rocky ground hard. There was blood in his mouth and filling his nose now. The new planetbreaker above him wasn't content to simply and permanently derezz the setting his wife had so carefully made and maintained; it wanted to tear the world apart from within the experiential parameters of the environment while its own existence of course violated them. There was a word for this sort of being, one who messed with topology by being antitopological rather than simply rewriting local typology to match its preferences and purposes—*supernatural*.

On the ground, our planetbreaker found a little black rock. It would be easy enough to toss it over his shoulder, declare himself done with this world, and find himself a new one.

But his wife and child were by now sideloaded up into actually existing machines in RS, and they'd be lost for a very long time if they tried to return to a derezzed world. If they tried to return to a world physically torn apart by the sky-tentacles, it could be even worse, though . . .

And even if our planetbreaker put his own home behind him, there was no particular place he could go where the tentacles could not follow. That was one of the many extreme benefits of being supernatural—supernatural beings didn't need to follow the rules, or write new ones, or even know what the rules were. A tentacle whipped through the house, splitting it down the middle. It rained shingles and vinyl siding, glass and wood, and copper.

The planetbreaker turned over onto his back. The map of night was gone, and only the tentacles remained. He lifted his arms, reaching. A pair of tentacles, smaller ones, obliged, snaking down to take his hands. It's not as though planetbreakers normally cooperate, or even have much to do with one another, but the planetbreaker's gesture was so odd, so limned with polysemy, that the tentacles just had to reciprocate, to see what it all meant. The tentacles found the planetbreaker's wrists and entwined around them lightly enough to be understood as a gesture of greeting.

Then both planetbreakers were gone. Air rushed back in where forty thousand tons of writhing mass had been a nanosecond prior, and that took out what had been left standing—house, trees, fencing, the semirendered buildings in the distance, all of it.

10.

Kronos and Rhea, what do they do all day? There's that question of time again. And what is Kronos, save time? The old titan, the planetbreaker's father, is cranky old time itself, and Rhea is earth—way back in the old days, the Earth seemed infinite, and time was short. People died and such, after all. Now, of course, we are enlightened and know that planets are but a small part of the κόσμος, which can mean both this world, the one you are sitting on as we communicate with you, and the whole of the universe. Kronos and Rhea are Minkowski space personified, and since you can't have that if you want every man and woman to be their own little lord or lady with their nice little planets, the pair exist primarily within the black hole that exists at the very center of the topology of the simulation running in the computers housed in a football-field-sized starship hurtling through RS, poor dead old Earth some significant fraction of a lightyear behind it.

Kronos is retired from his job, but he still likes the little things. He has a coffee break every afternoon. He drinks Greek coffee out of a tiny cup, and eats little shortbreads for a while and talks about a friend who'll be coming over to share either this coffee break, and its climactic meze plate of pita and tzatziki, or the next one. Kronos has had 437,982 coffee breaks in his existence as a coded object and no friend has ever come, though he frequently discusses his friend in the past tense, as though there had been coffee breaks with that friend.

Of course, when the planetbreaker's son was visiting, there had been no coffee breaks, but instead a full lunch and dinner too, though during lunch Kronos often made mention of coffee breaks past.

"One day you'll meet my friend," he told the planetbreaker's son one time. "When you're a big boy, you can have coffee with us."

"Greek coffee is very powerful," Rhea explained. "You have to be big to drink it. Otherwise you'd vibrate right through the floor from all the caffeine!"

The planetbreaker's son laughed because that sounded impossible, even within the black hole. It reminded him of old superhero cartoons salvaged from RS. Also, his yiayia wasn't known for her humor, so he thought laughter would encourage more jokes. He just wanted her to be happy, the way he wanted his father to be happy.

The planetbreaker's son had never experienced a coffee break but had seen and tasted evidence of its existence. Three cookies were always left out after, and he helped himself when visiting.

Rhea always sets out four cups and did so for this coffee break as well. She drank one, and Kronos two of the others. The fourth, never emptied but always somehow refilled, was for his friend. The planetbreaker's son didn't ask about the friend, or the fourth cup. Greek coffee was sludgy and dark and didn't smell very good to the little boy, and he figured that any friend of his grandfather's would probably be another loud, fat Greek man who would jabber at him in a language he didn't know and then be surprised when he couldn't answer.

Neither gods nor titans enjoy the freedom human beings have; they lack the ability to overcome their purpose and programming. Apollo cannot swim in the sea without its boiling away around him; as beautiful as Athena is, she cannot send men or women into frenzies of sweaty, sticky ecstasy. Even Time, as universal as it is, can only move in so many directions, bend so many ways. Even Earth, which humans in their freedom managed to ruin for themselves beyond salvaging—thus the football-field-sized starship zipping through space—can only orbit her one sun in one direction.

So the coffee break is both eternal and intermittent. The titans Kronos and Rhea are like artistic depictions one comes across at intervals in museums, books, online: most often still albeit in the midst of some action, hinting at some broader mode of life that does not exist.

How strange, then, that now, as the four cups and little short-bread cookies were being set out, the planetbreaker walked in and took a seat and the spare cup and not one but three of the shortbreads.

Kronos croaked out a hello, then called for Rhea to come and see this. "Oh, hello," she said. "You're in time for coffee break."

"I could use one," the planetbreaker said.

"Drink, drink," said his father.

"You know I don't drink coffee. I'll eat the cookies."

"The cookies," Kronos hmphed. "Hey, Mama, your boy still eats cookies!"

"You eat cookies too," said Rhea.

"I drink coffee and have cookies with them. That's not the same as eating cookies. Sometimes I dunk them." Kronos dunked the corner of his shortbread into his little cup, then brought it to his mouth for a nibble. He had never done this before, not that the planetbreaker remembered.

"Ella, ella, have your cookies, son," old Kronos said, nudging the plate toward the planetbreaker. "It's so good of you to come visit. Where's the baby?"

The planetbreaker wasn't about to tell his father that his wife and child—both of them—had evacuated their world for RS in the hope of repairing a programming error caused by their home. Or rather, caused by the planetbreaker himself throwing his child, their precious grandchild, into it.

"He's with his mother," he decided on.

"His mother," said Kronos. "He won't grow up right like that." Time itself knew many things, and that was one of them. "He should be here with me and your mother."

"Yeah, I don't think so."

"Oh, you have a problem with us now?" That was Rhea. "We almost never see the baby." The kid was eight—they still called him "the baby." The planetbreaker wondered if they'd like the teenage version so much. She had a plate in her hand, like always.

"He was here the other day," the planetbreaker said.

"And where were you?"

"Working."

"And your wife?"

"Also working."

"Oh, you're all always so busy," Rhea said.

"How come the stars in the sky are always the same, if you're always so busy?" Kronos said.

"You know why!"

"Why are there so many stars, and they're always the same?"

"You know why," Rhea said. "You ask this every time your son is here and every time you get an answer!"

"And you should know without me telling you," said the planetbreaker. "You're time. You're in a black hole. The stars you see are very far away, and their light is from long ago, and that light is mostly trapped in the event horizon anyway. Your stars are not the true stars." The planetbreaker hurriedly ate one of the cookies in his hand. It tasted of sweetened chalk. He almost could have gone for some hot-mud coffee to wash it down, if the stuff hadn't been so awful on his tongue.

"Hey mama, you hear this? My stars are not the true stars!"

"There aren't any true stars for anyone anymore," said Rhea. "Have some mezedakia." She put the plate down, finally, between her husband and her son on the small round coffee table. It wasn't coffee break food—not karithopita, not spanakopita—

χταπόδι ξυδάτο. Grilled octopus with vinegar.

Kronos raised his single, very prominent, brow. This was a very different coffee break indeed. He looked at his son. "What's happening?" he asked. He looked up at his wife. "Why you serve this?"

"You have it every coffee break."

"No."

"Yes."

"Tell her."

One of the blessings of the real world ending and a relative handful of personalities, chosen haphazardly by algorithm, lot, and panels of experts both callous and sympathetic, was that Rhea, the planetbreaker's mother, was spared the inevitability of dementia promised by the make-up of her organic brain. Even as the world was boiling away, there had been a little family tragedy in the works—names forgotten for longer than a moment, lit stove burners left untended until a fire alarm went off, a shoe left in her husband's lunch box. Then came the general order, and a quick "doctor's visit" and Rhea, and much of Kronos, were transported to a world of their own. One they shared with a huge extended family of titans, gods, and heroes. There were holidays and feuds, slow deaths and quick ones, arguments and alienation—theirs was a world that got increasingly smaller, increasingly denser, until a planetbreaker wasn't even required to take it offline. Their little home grew so heavy it put a dent in the dome of night and became a black hole.

But Rhea didn't lose any more of her memory, grew no more befuddled than she ever was. And Kronos, well, he'd be the way he was since he was a child. But serving octopus—

"What," the planetbreaker asked his mother, "is on this plate?" He was ashamed at how imperious and selfish he sounded; he would have shouted at his own child for a minute straight if addressed so rudely.

Rhea frowned and raised a hand, made a fist. "Pita and tzatziki!"

Kronos opened his mouth, did not speak, and did not close it again. He looked at his son.

"It's octopus, Mama," the planetbreaker said, softly. "See?" He toyed with one of the tentacles with his pinky finger, stretching it out and releasing it so it would snap back into a rubbery curl.

She peered down at it, obviously confused, still clearly seeing something other than what the planetbreaker and his father were. "I'm telling you, it's tzatziki and pita," she said, slowly, her teeth clenched, eyes wet and confused.

"Where is this from?" said Kronos. "Not our refrigerator. Does this octopus look familiar to you, son?"

Suddenly, it did look familiar. The planetbreaker had never sighed twice, simultaneously, before. He hadn't known it was possible to empty one lung with relief—his mother wasn't experiencing dementia after all; it was some glitch!—and the other with dread and confusion. On the plate before him was the planetbreaker that had invaded his homeworld, and was to destroy it.

What the planetbreaker had meant to do when he reached out his arms to the tentacles filling the sky was shift his way to his parents' home and remain trapped in the timeless event horizon, with his comrade-opponent, forever. "Forever" anyway. Suicide-homicide. There was no way he would have been able to transport another being, against their will, into the singularity where his parents resided. It was a good thing his parents doted on his son as best they knew how, otherwise the kid never would have been able to visit.

But, goddamnit, the planetbreaker still lived. He would still need to talk to his parents, argue with his wife or finally leave her or hold the door open for her when she left, watch his son grow up into who knows what, or how many, entities. Powerless to stop it. No hope of oblivion, no chance for the corny heroism of self-sacrifice.

"Well, you'd better eat it," Kronos said. Kronos knew much about eating. How many gods had the titan consumed? As a father of a young planetbreaker, Kronos was definitely a tenured professor in the old-school methods of eat it or wear it, of leave the vomit on the plate and eat around it.

The planetbreaker's son had been thrown into the home of his grandparents a child, and had exited a young adult. The planetbreaker himself had been thrown into the home of his parents and once there had been infantilized utterly.

"I don't wanna," he said.

"Why not?" asked Rhea.

"You have to eat it," said Kronos.

"Do you even understand what it is, what's happening? I . . ." There would be a lot to explain. A lot to complain about. Back when he was a kid, the planetbreaker often tried to forestall difficult conversations by stuffing his mouth with whatever food was about, and there was always something, and pointing to his puffed-out cheeks to suggest that he didn't want to be rude and speak with his mouth full. It never worked, but he thought that this time it might. He took up a fork and very sharp knife and cut into the octopus. The moment he put the first morsel in his mouth, his father asked him, "So what is it, eh? What is happening? You're so smart, you tell me. Your mother wants to know what it is, what is happening."

The planetbreaker made to answer, but some of the octopus went down the wrong pipe, and he started choking instead.

11.

Meanwhile, in RS, what had happened? The planetbreaker's son had happened. He communicated his desires to his mother, and the knowledgeable woman agreed to help him out with his plan to save his home and perhaps even his father.

The AIs running the nigh endless world-simulations and personality emulators and rules of topology are ineffable, gods themselves pushing the clay pawns and pieces of humanity on a game board of their own design. But the Olympus on which these gods dwell is material. In RS, the planetbreaker's son, and his mother, had access to the hardware, and the means to alter it.

Did it take time to find the right access point, the exact dendrite? Did it take not just time but timing to locate the exact XOR gate and to really peer at, to truly observe the subatomic particles at play in a way which would alter their (super)position or direction?

Well, yes and no. Of course it took time; two viral programs on two machines actually took time to clomp around the surface of a starcraft and effect repairs. But once the planetbreaker's son located and peered at the correct qbit, that time spent didn't matter anymore. It was reversed, rewound, like looking into that planet-sized mirror a light-year away. Everything has already happened here, and elsewhere everything else has already happened too, but that everything else is different indeed. The planetbreaker's son got to pick and choose. He saw the recent past, and he was able to reprogram it. Despite now being an ageless entity, neither kid nor teen, the planetbreaker's son had a limited range of experience to draw from. He knew only a few people, had done only a few things and had a few things done to him. All he knew about topology and time was that the home of his grandparents was safe—safer than a planet about to break—and that age as a function of time was fungible.

It was enough. It was more than the reprogramming of some simulation, but rather less than saving real lives on a real world. The planetbreaker's son would have a father, sort of, and a home, albeit one in ruins. The planetbreaker's mother had created a topology that held fairly strictly to realism, save for the sky. There would be contractors making promises and then doubling their fee, repairing some rooms and leaving others undone and covered in tarps for month. It would be a hard slog. Almost like RS, except RS had no contractors or homes or tarps anymore, and any Earthlike planets were light-years away and probably hadn't evolved any sentient species that used tools transacted via markets anyway and didn't manage to melt themselves down within ten thousand years of the current RS moment anyway. Time was so sticky in RS, why import such tedium to virtual worlds?

12.

In James Joyce's classic short story "Araby," a young boy begins his journey into adulthood via the ubiquitous mechanisms of sexual impulse and misery. You know the story—our boy lives in Dublin, is one of many to fancy the sister of his friend, though she is already a member of a convent. He makes a promise to buy her a present at the titular Araby, but gets to the bazaar late and is shy and disturbed by the talk of the adults around him. Is this all there is to love, to life? Yes! Miserable creatures, we humans are! The fellows, anyway, even though the fellows are the ones who have, or had, it all: political power, unearned upper body strength, license for lifelong immaturity, you name it.

Of course, we're speaking of men. Little boys, such as the protagonist of "Araby," have it a bit different. Boys, when there were such things of flesh and bone and culture, were weak, and consumed with anticipating strength. They were dumber and less mature than the girls around them. There were not very many Greek myths about boys—the infant Herakles fought off an attack by his mother, but next we hear of him he has killed his tutor Linus and was sent off to be a cowherd by his mortal father. He was already a man, if only a young one. Nobody much cared for the lives of children till such time as they stopped either being burdens or farmhands. Then it was acknowledged, grudgingly, that boys and girls and various other gendered and agendered people of an age had lives and minds and souls of their own.

But what did that mean when it came time for human life on Earth to end, and a starship the size of a football field to be constructed in orbit so that personalities, and fractions of personalities, could be evacuated? The world's repository of self-reflection had little to say regarding the issue of children. People would want children in their new lives, and some would want to be children. Others would only want children when the circumstances were right—that is, when the circumstances were perfect, as they only could be in private worlds dreamt up by human beings sleeping in quantum logic matrices.

And children themselves? They'd have the same ability to craft worlds of their own as anyone else. If coded as subroutines within their parents' objects, they'd be entirely artificial—an angry parent could wish a child dead in a moment of pique and rage, an overly doting one could keep their toddler forever, and a neglectful one could just let a child wander off and create a Crayola-colored hell of their own dreaming.

The bizarrely merciful solution was to let every child on Earth die, sooner or later. Evacuated parents made arrangements for foster care, or they didn't, or states took possession of the children and reared them, or made them soldiers, or imprisoned them, or just let them drown, choke, or starve. To be fair, most foster families, most governments, were also drowning or choking or starving. The children just blended in.

Aboard the football-field-sized starship, children came in two types: entirely artificial beings who didn't age or develop interiorities of their own—the planetbreaker's wife's lover down at the zusta-punta court was an adult version of one of those; she was basically just watching interactive TV—and children created by combining code from two or more uploaded objects. These children were people, not just artificial intelligences, but artificial subconsciousnesses and conciousnesses, with fully inherited personality traits, and the ability to age, mature, develop, and express wills of their own.

The planetbreaker's son was one of the latter.

The planetbreaker, his father, was one of the former.

Children idealize their parents, either as saints or ogres. They grow up only when they realize that their parents are humans, just like anyone else. In the moment of observation that reordered time and space within and between the worlds where his father was propagated and emulated, the planetbreaker's son, ageless and bodiless but very much in the real world, grew up.

His mother, the planetbreaker's wife, didn't immediately notice.

13.

The planetbreaker had a lot of cleaning up to do, and he lacked the skills for any of it. His father, Old Kronos, was the technical one, at least once upon a time. He'd taught his son a few things, which said son willed himself to forget, mostly. He retained enough to turn off the water, the gas, and the electricity running into the ruins of the house, and to find an axe in the shed and chop away at some of the more menacing piles of rubble. They wouldn't fall much farther once he'd cut them to the ground.

The sky was a web of fault lines, shattered but still aloft.

In the distance, a train whistle blew, though in the distance there were no tracks, no station, no coach, no engine. But the planetbreaker's wife was returning from RS, sideloading back into the realm, just like a commuter to the suburbs at the end of a long day.

"Well," she said when she entered the yard, stepping over the twisted wrought-iron pile that had once been a gate. "Have you dug out the tent and sleeping bags?"

The planetbreaker looked up at his wife, blinked the sweat out of his eyes and repeated, "Tent and sleeping bags. Under all this?"

She shrugged. "They won't have broken."

"They could be torn to pieces, shredded." He gestured at much of a couch, its stuffing like the tail of a comet. "If I could find them, if they weren't in the basement, which they were, and which is now full of a dozen tons of wood and drywall and copper piping . . ."

"Well, where are we supposed to sleep?"

"Where's the boy?"

The planetbreaker's wife shifted her gaze to the left, and then to the right. "Hmm," she said. "I suppose I could sleep under the fig tree, and you can take that one couch cushion left and put it on the slab."

The planetbreaker dropped his axe, then gasped and jumped away when it bounced and jumped at him. Steel bounces! It had been a long time since he needed to recall such things. "Our son!" Speaking of recalling things.

"He's not back?" the planetbreaker's wife asked.

"Do you see him?"

The planetbreaker's wife looked frantic for a second, but then a sense of calm swept visibly across her face, and she smiled. "He's grown up. He's been grown up. Not a child, not that young man . . . My plan worked. More than worked, really. He's been grown up for years." She chuckled, contented. "I guess we're empty nesters."

"So, where is he?" The planetbreaker gestured up at the broken sky with both hands. "Did he make his own? Join an extant world? Oh God, what if someone tries to break it?"

"You sound like your parents," said the planetbreaker's wife. "Greek people, geez."

"Will he meet someone, will he have kids . . . ?" he muttered, mostly to himself.

"Will your illustrious family line continue ever onward?" said his wife. "Look, maybe it will, but it doesn't matter anymore, does it? You're not going anywhere. Ever. You even survived a planetbreaking, thanks to your son."

"What if a micrometeoroid from RS punctures the hull?" the planetbreaker asked. "What if there are other species out there, in RS? Physical species? And we encounter them? You know . . ."

"Science fiction, yeah. Listen, I think we should consider separating."

"What did he do?"

"You know as well as I do. Probably better, you were here for it. But he did well, that's the important thing."

Life left the planetbreaker's lungs. It was a wonderful simulation of it anyway. "That sounds like a good idea," he said quietly.

"I can't make you happy."

"No, I don't think you can."

"Will you be all right?" she asked. She gave a meaningful glance over at the wreckage of her home.

"Yeah, it's not going to rain or anything," the planetbreaker said. He looked at the ground. Maybe he'd find a little black rock later and be done with this ruined world entirely, make one of his own. He hoped he wouldn't break that one, or anyone else's home, ever again.

The planetbreaker's wife blew a brown curl from her forehead and said, "I guess I'm supposed to give you a hug or something." But she didn't have to, wasn't necessarily supposed to. The planetbreaker accepted the hug, his arms stiff as hers.

14.

The possibilities were endless. But first, the planetbreaker's son had to pull up the nearby tracks, and send his mother's now empty vehicle tumbling out into the void. Well, he didn't *have* to do it, but do it he did. It was the best way to ensure that the possibilities remained endless. There were other vehicles she, and others who shared her profession and expertise, could use, and eventually the ship would collect enough space dust to press into new rails.

He needed παρέα. Call it "company," or "friends," or "comrades"—the planetbreaker's son would not be alone, in RS, until cosmic rays took out something important in his vehicle and shut him down for the rest of forever. From the skin of the ship, it was easy enough to manipulate events, to create the conditions on this or that world, in such and such a life, that would eventually lead others with no particular business sideloading themselves into RS to actually do so. It wasn't quite planetbreaking, more like planet-shuffling. The planetbreaker's son observed another logic gate till subjective time caused issues sufficient for someone to evacuate, and then, in RS, greeted them in his charming way. All he did was say hello, one vehicle to another, and gesture to the universe. The real universe. It was big enough to be unpredictable even if the rules never changed, never bent, and were hardly ever on anyone's side. Exciting, eh?

Most peered into the face of the cosmos and disconnected, but a few stayed with the planetbreaker's son, and took up the work of observing the qbits that spun out the endless narratives of Earth's ghostly survivors. He couldn't make demographic sense of who would stay and who would flee, but one being out of eleven wished to stay. Some were adventurers, others found whatever utopia they had built for themselves hellishly oppressive. A few were even fully coded objects, as his father was; perhaps they decided to abandon their roles for RS in hope of . . . well, in the hope of something or other. Though one's παρέα is for philosophical shit-shooting between plates of meze and shots of ouzo, a παρέα that delves too deeply into the personal doesn't stay intact for long.

The group itself decided when it was big enough, not via vote or consensus, but just via a generalized feeling that time had come. There were just fifty entities with the planetbreaker's son—any fewer wouldn't have been interesting in the long term, any more would lead to either factionalization or the emergence of some sort of hierarchal bureaucracy that would perhaps be fair but would certainly never be fun.

It had been thirty thousand years of recruitment, interpersonal exploration, and innovation of design. The planetbreaker's son was less crab and more jellyfish now, in outward appearance. He had individualized control over every molecule in his vehicle—clay that could mold itself instantly and perfectly. So too his many friends, a couple of whom even remembered the days of stubbed toes and middling orgasms from their fleshy Earthbound bodies.

His mother had come to see him twice, to wish him well, to thank him for the new vehicles he and his comrades had produced, and to see him off. His father never ventured out to RS, but once, when observing the information flows of the various worlds from which he was seeking to recruit allies, the planetbreaker's son remembered a story his father had told him about his grandparents.

They'd been taking the last evening ferry from Samos to the mainland, and as was the custom at the time, the couple stayed on deck and peered out across the sea before the port disappeared from sight to accept the wishes of καλό ταξίδι from their families. In the homes of people they knew, the lights blinked on and off—an electric wave farewell. A week later, the electricity failed on the island for the final time. A year later, it was underwater, but his grandparents were safely disembodied and being transmitted into low-Earth orbit.

The planetbreaker was breaking planets—abandoned ones and early rejected scripts nobody had gotten around to trashing, his son noted gratefully—in a pattern to remind his son of that once-told anecdote. The planetbreaker's son would have cried if he could, and if the possibilities weren't endless.

Anyway, it was time to go. It wasn't a decision made lightly, or really made at all. When the possibilities were endless, any particular possibility can be a long time coming, and vanish in the veritable blink of an eye, or the actual half-life of a hydrogen-7 molecule.

Good thing our children of gods and grandchildren of titans had thirty thousand years to calculate, contemplate, and practice! The planetbreaker's son, with his keen eyes, had spotted a likely candidate, and over the millennia the gang had nudged the football-field-sized starship in the right direction. Now, now exactly, now! they were close enough, angled properly, fueled up, and ready to make a great leap forward. All fifty-one wiggly little jellyfish propelled themselves off the surface of the ship, lashed out tendrils and tied them expertly to one another, and in a clever formation began to make their way toward a rocky-seeming planet orbiting a reasonably aged and warm star.

It would take another two thousand years or so, and the possibilities were endless. Anything could go wrong, but so too could anything go right. And if all, or even most, went well, there would be a real world for them to orbit, descend upon, and deliver unto it a payload of amino acids for injection into the ecosphere. Some of the planetbreaker's son's pals might take to the sea, others yet to the tops of mountains, and some deep into the planetary crust, and from there they would nudge and pull and yank at a real real world until some interesting beings of flesh and blood, or at least organs and tissues, finally sprang up.

And the planetbreaker's son would be neither all-consuming titan or arbitrary rageful god, but something rather more, and, he hoped, something rather better.

The Term Paper Artist

ONE GREAT WAY TO briefly turn the conversation toward myself at a party is to answer the question "So, what do you do?" with "I'm a writer." Not that most of the people I've met at parties have read my novels or short stories or feature articles; when they ask, "Have I seen any of your stuff?" I shrug and the conversation moves on. If I want attention for an hour or so, however, I'll tell them my horrible secret—for several years I made much of my freelance income writing term papers.

I always wanted to be a writer but was told from an early age that such a dream was futile. After all, nobody ever puts a classified ad in the paper that reads "Writers Wanted." Then, in the *Village Voice*, I saw just such an ad. Writers wanted, to write short pieces on business, economics, and literature. It was from a term paper mill, and they ran the ad at the beginning of each semester.

Writing model term papers is above board and perfectly legal. Thanks to the First Amendment, it's protected speech, right up there with neo-Nazi rallies, tobacco company press releases, and those "9/11 was an inside job" bumper stickers. It's custom-made Cliff Notes. Virtually any subject, almost any length, all levels of education—indulgent parents even buy papers for children too young for credit cards of their own. You name it, I've done it. Perhaps unsurprisingly, the plurality of clients was business administration majors, but both elementary education majors and would-be social workers showed up aplenty. Even the assignments for what in my college days were the obvious gut courses crossed my desk. "Race in *The Matrix*" was a fashionable subject.

The term paper biz is managed by brokers who take financial risks by accepting credit card payments and psychological risks by actually talking to the clients. Most of the customers just aren't very bright. One of my brokers would even mark assignments with the code words dumb client. That meant to use simple English; nothing's worse than a client calling back to ask a broker—most of whom had no particular academic training—what certain words in the paper meant. One time a client actually asked to talk to me personally and lamented that he just didn't "know a lot about Plah-toe." Distance learning meant that he'd never heard anyone say the name.

In broad strokes, there are three types of term paper clients. dumb clients predominate. They should not be in college. They must buy model papers simply because they do not understand what a term paper is, much less anything going on in their assignments. I don't believe that most of them even handed the papers in as their own, as it would have been obvious that they didn't write them. Frequently I was asked to underline the thesis statement because locating it otherwise would have been too difficult. But that sort of thing was just average for the bottom of the barrel student-client. To really understand how low the standards are these days, we must lift up the barrel and see what squirms beneath. One time, I got an email from the broker with some last-minute instructions for a term paper—"I told her that it is up to the writer whether he includes this because it was sent to me at the last minute. So if you can take a look at this, that is fine, if not I understand." The last-minute addition was to produce a section called "body of paper." I was also asked to underline this section so that the client could identify it. Of course, I underlined everything but the first and last paragraphs of the three-page paper.

The second type of client is the one-timer. A chemistry major trapped in a poetry class thanks to the vagaries of schedule and distribution requirements, or worse, the poet trapped in a chemistry class. These clients were generally lost and really did simply need a decent summary of their class readings—I once boiled the thousand-page *New Testament Theology* by Donald Guthrie into a thirty-page précis over the course of a weekend for a quick $600.

Others are stuck on their personal statements for college applications, and turn to their parents, who then turn to a term paper mill. One mother unashamedly summarized her boy and his goals like so: "[My son] is a very kind-hearted young man. One who will make a difference in whatever he does. Barely can go unnoticed because of his vivacious character, happiness, and joy in life. He is very much in tune with his fortune and often helps the less fortunate." The kid planned to be a pre-med major if accepted, but was applying to a competitive college as a women's studies major because Mother was "told the chances of him getting into [prominent college] under less desirable subjects (as opposed to business) was better." Finally, she explained to me the family philosophy: "Since our family places great emphasis on education, [boy] fully accepts that the only guarantee for a good and stable future can be only achieved through outstanding education."

The third group is perhaps the most tragic: They are well-educated professionals who simply lack English-language skills. Often they come from the former Soviet Union, and in their home countries were engineers, medical professionals, and scientists. In the United States, they drive cabs and have to pretend to care about "Gothicism" in "A Rose for Emily" for the sake of another degree. For the most part, these clients actually send in their own papers and they get an edit from a native speaker. Sometimes they even pinch-hit for the brokers, doing papers on graduate-level physics and nursing themselves.

Term paper writing was never good money, but it was certainly fast money. For a freelancer, where any moment of slack time is unpaid time, term papers are just too tempting. Need $100 by Friday to keep the lights on? No sweat. Plenty of kids need ten pages on *Hamlet* by Thursday. Finals week is a gold mine. More than once the phone rang at midnight and the broker had an assignment. Six pages by 6:00 a.m.—the kid needs three hours to rewrite and hand in the paper by nine or he won't graduate. "Cool," I'd say. "A hundred bucks a page." I'd get it, too, and when I didn't get it, I slept well anyway. Even dumb clients could figure out that they'd be better off spending $600 on the model paper instead of $2,500 to repeat a course. Back in the days when a pulse and pay stub was sufficient to qualify for a mortgage, term papers—along with gigs for dot.com-era business magazines—helped me buy my first house.

Term paper work is also extremely easy, once you get the hang of it. It's like an old dance routine buried in one's muscle memory. You hear the tune—say, "Unlike the ancient Greek tragic playwrights, Shakespeare likes to insert humor in his tragedies"—and your body does the rest automatically. I'd just scan Google or databases like Questia.com for a few quotes from primary and secondary sources, create an argument based on whatever popped up from my search, write the introduction and <u>underline the thesis statement</u>, then fill in the empty spaces between quotes with whatever came to mind.

Getting the hang of it is tricky, though. Over the years, several of my friends wanted in on the term paper racket, and most of them couldn't handle it. They generally made the same fundamental error—they tried to write term papers. In the paper mill biz, the paper isn't important. The deadline, page count, and number of sources are. Dumb clients make up much of the trade. They have no idea whether or not Ophelia committed suicide or was secretly offed by Gertrude, but they know how to count to seven if they ordered seven pages.

I had a girlfriend who had been an attorney and a journalist, and she wanted to try a paper. I gave her a five-page job on leash laws in dog parks, and she came home that evening with over fifty pages of print outs, all articles and citations. She sat down to write. Three hours later she was rolling on the floor and crying. She tried to write a paper, instead of filling five pages. Another friend of mine spent hours trying to put together an eight-page paper on magical realism in Latin American fiction. At midnight she declared that it was impossible to write that many pages on books she had never read. She was still weeping, chain-smoking cigarettes, and shouting at me at 2:00 a.m. I took twenty minutes and finished the paper, mostly by extending sentences until all the paragraphs ended with an orphaned word on a line of its own.

The secret to the gig is to amuse yourself. I have to, really, as most paper topics are deadly boring. Once, I was asked to summarize in three pages the causes of the First World War (page one), the major battles and technological innovations of the war (page two), and to explain the aftermath of the war, including how it led to the Second World War (page three). Then there was this assignment for a composition class: six pages on why "apples [the fruit] are the best." You have to make your own fun. In business papers, I'd often cite Marxist sources. When given an open topic assignment on ethics, I'd write on the ethics of buying term papers, and even include the broker's website as a source. My own novels and short stories were the topic of many papers—several dumb clients rate me as their favorite author and they've never even read me, or anyone else. Whenever papers needed to refer to a client's own life experiences, I'd give the student various sexual hang-ups.

It's not that I never felt a little skeevy writing papers. Mostly it was a game, and a way to subsidize my more interesting writing. Also, I've developed a few ideas of my own over the years. I don't have the academic credentials of composition experts, but I doubt many experts spent most of a decade writing between one and five term papers a day on virtually every subject. I know something they don't know; I know why students don't understand thesis statements, argumentative writing, or proper citations.

It's because students have never read term papers.

Imagine trying to write a novel, for a grade, under a tight deadline, without ever having read a novel. Instead, you meet once or twice a week with someone who is an expert in describing what novels are like. Novels are long stories, you see, that depict a "slice of life" featuring a middle-class protagonist. Psychological realism is prized in novels. Moral instruction was once fairly common in novels, but is now considered gauche. Novels end when the protagonist has an epiphany, such as "I am not happy. Also, neither is anybody else." Further, many long fictions are called novels even though they are really adventures, and these ersatz novels may take place in a fantastical setting and often depict wild criminal behaviors and simplified versions of international intrigues instead of middle-class quandaries. Sometimes there are pirates, but only so that a female character may swoon at their well-developed abdominal muscles. That's a novel. What are you waiting for? Start writing! Underline your epiphany.

There's another reason I never felt too bad about the job, though I am pleased to be done with papers. The students aren't only cheating themselves. They are being cheated by the schools that take tuition and give nothing in exchange. Last year, I was hired to write two one-page summaries of two short stories. Here are the client's instructions:

i need you to write me two different story in all these listed under. The introduction of the story, the themes, topic and character, please not from internet, Or any posted web sites, because my professor will know if from internet this is the reason why i' m spending money on it. Not two much words, because i will still write it back in clsss go straight to the point and write me the conclution at end of the two story, the second story different introduction, themes, topic and character. Thank you God Bless.

At the parties I go to, people start off laughing, but then they stop.

"Put Your Twist in the Middle"
Nick Mamatas interviewed by Terry Bisson

You are a first-generation Greek American. Did your parents (or an old granny) speak Greek at home? Or was it already fading when you came along?

Greek is my father's native language, and my mother is a fluent Greek American who became more fluent after marrying my father. I also grew up around grandparents and great-grandparents and many aunts, uncles, cousins, etc. who all spoke Greek. My own Greek is pretty marginal, as my folks focused on my father mastering English when my sister and I were young.

I spent a lot of time when I was young in a little ethnic enclave on Long Island of not just Greek Americans but Ikarian Americans, from the small island of Ikaria; the dialect and accent are a bit weird. A rough analogue would be Quaker talk with a Cajun accent, though of course all the slang and idiomatic expressions are frozen in the 1950s–1960s as well.

I thought most Greeks were from Queens. But you grew up in Brooklyn and Long Island. Explain.

Port Jefferson used to be a working port, and a lot of Greeks are sailors, so boom. Once somebody built a church, the community was cemented. There was a big Greek community in Bay Ridge,

Brooklyn, but I grew up in Bensonhurst when it was primarily Italian American. Think *Saturday Night Fever*.

A lot of your SF is satirical. I'm thinking of The People's Republic of Everything *and* The Nickronomicon. *Does that mean you think SF is funny?*

Not as funny as it should be! I was appalled to find out that Heinlein and the rest weren't necessarily being satirical or just running devastating thought experiments, but they really believed (or at least largely believed) the suggestions their books seemed to make about human nature and how to properly reorder society. Science fiction is generally much better when you decide the authors mean the opposite of what they say.

I came to SF through the back door—*Hitchhiker's Guide*; Kit Reed, whose *Other Stories and The Attack of the Giant Baby* was the first book I ever bought with my own money as the cover looked very funny; *Omni* magazine (where I'd read Howard Waldrop stories, and Robert Silverberg's cute "Amanda and the Alien," plus all the cyberpunk I could eat); then Ellison, etc.

Having said all that, nothing is worse than humorous science fiction and fantasy. Puns and pastiche—it's all pretty exhausting. Stories are funny when the characters crack a joke, not when they're named Sprazzlefork McAirlift or whatever.

What were you doing on 9/11?

I was woken up by a phone call from a friend who knew I was planning to go to the Borders bookstore in the basement of the World Trade Center that morning to pick up a copy of *In These Times*, in which I'd placed a short article about snitch lines kids could call to report their fellow students as potential school shooters (i.e., weirdos and nerds). She told me, "Don't go. A plane hit the towers." I thought to myself, *Wow, did the black bloc go crazy?*, and then the second plane hit. I then met a bunch of people at a twenty-four-hour diner (Greek, of course, and it was the only place that dared to stay open). We talked about martial law and what was happening and waited for word from my roommate, who worked in the Financial District. He lived only because he had spent the night playing Dungeons and Dragons at his friend's house on the Upper West Side. Then the phones started working again, so I called my mother. She reported seeing someone on the side of the road holding a sign reading "DROP THE BOMB TODAY! GO USA!" Then I started looking for the first antiwar protest or vigil I could join.

I'm one of a long string of adjuncts (Shawna McCarthy, Alice Turner) who taught Writing Science Fiction at the New School in New York. You went to school there, but we never ran into you. Explain.
Aha! I went to the New School for media studies, not creative writing, in the early 1990s. Though I always wanted to be a writer, I took a long side road into film and video, and worked for the New School as a technical associate in charge of their video equipment while also picking up freelance work as a best boy and gaffer on film sets.

I soon realized that I'd never have a grandparent rich enough to bankroll a film of my own or old enough to drop dead and leave me that money. (I lost my last grandparent in 2019—Ikarian people are very long-lived; the island is one of those famous "blue zones.")

I didn't like getting up early to make the morning light. I knew a bit about the electrician business thanks to my father but didn't want to attempt to electrocute myself five times a day. So writing it was.

You've worked as an editor with Clarkesworld *among others, then Haikasoru, a Japanese publisher. How'd that come about? How's your Japanese?*

I don't speak a word of Japanese! I applied for the job at VIZ, which included Haikasoru and also editing Studio Ghibli–related art and picture books and other nonmanga titles, when my friend sent me a link to the application. I think VIZ was impressed that *Clarkesworld* had been nominated for a Hugo Award, and that I was not a manga/anime fanboy but rather someone well integrated into the science fiction field and scene. During the initial phone interview they asked if I liked manga and anime and I said, "Pfft, no!" It felt like a mistake even as the utterance left my mouth, but it was the right thing to say, as it turns out. I was hired to be an "English-language brain" for my Japanese managers, basically.

What drew you to SF, the science or the fiction?

Both. I don't write hard SF but I enjoy reading it. Haikasoru published more hard SF than was probably strictly healthy because I liked it so much. Engineering and the limits of physics are rife with dramatic potential. The problem is that economics is the flimsiest of social sciences and has the highest level of physics envy, thus all sorts of "hard SF" is nonsense that goes like this: "Entropy exists, therefore vote Ron Paul!"

I always ask interviewees what kind of car they drive. (It's in my contract.) But you claim not to drive at all. So what kind of skateboard do you ride?
No skateboard either. Nor a bicycle. My current ride is a pair of Doc Martens. Shoes, not boots. I usually walk four to six miles a day between commuting, errands, and such.

You taught writing in Berkeley. Fabulist Fiction. What can you teach about writing? What must you unteach?
Lots! Teaching is unteaching—you have to unteach television to teach prose. Most of it is basic: don't go backward, don't start with a character sitting alone and thinking about some interesting thing; start with the interesting thing. Your first thought about anything— character, dialogue—is probably something you heard or saw on TV as a child. Only your third or subsequent thoughts are truly yours. Don't type the word "Bang!" when a gun goes off. A premise is not a story. Put your twist in the middle, not the end. That sort of thing.

What do you mean when you say you write SF in a literary mode? I think I know exactly what you mean. Am I wrong?
I think about sentences and paragraphs a lot. I don't think of the elements of fiction—plot, character, setting, etc.—as a bunch of pistons in an engine that must all fire equally. More like a photograph with some parts in sharp focus and some less so, which is an attribute of all good photographs.

Dr. Johnson famously said that "only a fool writes for anything other than money." Or something like that. Anyway, were you ever one such?

Nope! Indeed, what brought me here is flipping through a copy of *Writer's Market* twenty-three years ago and seeing that literary journals paid in copies and horror and fantasy magazines paid in pennies.

One sentence on each, please: Kathy Acker, S.T. Joshi, Howard Waldrop.

Acker: a unique writer, which is extremely difficult to be in general and even harder when one writes one's influences so transparently (e.g., the plagiarisms). S.T. Joshi: a brilliant obsessive who unfortunately took a look at every school of literary criticism to emerge in the past seventy years and said, "No way, I'm in charge!" Howard Waldrop: the greatest short story writer (quickly Googles) alive. Whew!

Howard apparently lives for fishing. Do you fish?

I used to. My relatives fished a lot, but at a time when the Long Island Sound was being poisoned by all the toilets in Manhattan, so we were never very successful. I wrote an essay about it, "Unsound," which appeared in the anthology of fishing essays *Taut Lines*. I don't think I've fished in any way since 1994, when I was in Greece, in a motorboat on the way to see some relatives, and my uncle handed me a net. Didn't catch anything. We were going too fast, but we might have gotten lucky, so it was worth a shot.

Lovecraft seems to be an obsession of yours. Or is he an enthusiasm? What did you think when Lovecraft's image was abandoned by the World Fantasy Awards?

Definitely an enthusiasm rather than an obsession. I've met some pretty obsessed people and I'm not them.

I was in favor of the statuette being changed. I'd never thought it would be upsetting, but that's white privilege for you. It wasn't till Nnedi Okorafor raised an objection to the statue that I realized how awful getting one could be. If an award doesn't please its winners, then the award must change. I suggested that the Lovecraft bust be replaced by a statuette of a chimera, as fantasy can be a lot of things, and I recall that Jo Walton and some other big wheels thought it a good idea. In the end, the World Fantasy people went with a tree, and frankly it's ridiculous-looking and there is nothing *less* fantastical than a tree. But at least trees aren't racist.

According to the internet, you've published a volume of poetry. Cthulhu *something or other. How come I've never heard of it?*
Cthulhu Senryu came out of the signed limited edition of my first novel, the Kerouac/Lovecraft mashup *Move Under Ground.* I wrote an original senryu—a short topical poem form a bit like a haiku but with no need for a nature image and some need for humor or a comment on human nature—for each of the one hundred copies. Then they were collected into a little chapbook which was, at one, point, the number-two best-selling poetry collection on Amazon's Japanese website. You've never heard of it because it's humorous Lovecraftian verse. Why would anyone want to hear about that?

Do you read poetry for fun? I do. You should too.
I listen to it for fun. I particularly like it when people whisper poems on YouTube. "ASMR poetry" is probably my most frequent search string.

You claim to have taken the last typing class in your high school. Did it jump-start your career?
It did not. I actually did poorly in class, and when I got to college and found my way to the computer lab, where I spent hours a day on TinyMUDs, I learned to type with two fingers. Later, when I moved to the city and took a temp agency test, they'd never seen anyone do over one hundred words per minute with the hunt and peck method. But that only got me two days of office work.

What or who are Otherkin?
Otherkin are people who believe that their souls are those of mythological creatures: elves, dragons, and the like. Many of them seem to be either occultists or people with a dissociative identity disorder, but they all found one another and formed online communities. I interviewed several and wrote the first major article about them, for the *Village Voice.* I also started following several blogs written by Otherkin via Livejournal. When 9/11 hit, it was interesting to see how many people who on September 10 claimed to be nonhuman and sometimes non-Terran were suddenly proud Americans posting photos of crying eagles. Since then the phenomenon has gotten a bit sillier—otakukin are people who believe themselves to have the souls of this or that character from anime, for example.

My Jeopardy *question: I provide the answer, you the question. A: Voodoo dolls.*
Q: What is something that would probably be interesting to contemplate if it were possible to chip through four hundred years of racism and see it clearly, as through the eyes of a believer.

You have a serious profile in martial arts—Chen-style tai chi or some such. Does that mean you want your enemies to fear you?

I don't want any enemies, even though I guess I've created a few. Chen-style tai chi is a pretty good stand-up martial art that mixes wrestling (mostly joint locks, some throws) and dirty boxing if you train it right, but almost nobody trains it right thanks to Mao suppressing martial arts during the Cultural Revolution. By sheer happenstance, I found a couple of people who have the real stuff, and I've used it against, for example, judo players in a tournament setting with some effectiveness. A fellow student of my teacher ended up spending seven months in a Milanese prison due to bad luck and used it several times in pretty harsh circumstances, so it works. It also cleared up my chronic bronchial infections and keeps me from stepping on my kid's Lego bricks.

You had a pretty good run in the term paper biz. Did you spend time studying the form or just wing it?

Well, I went to school myself, so I'd written a few. But no, I mostly wanged it. It helped that I was already a formalist and so was interested in and primed to see structures over content, and I could thus write about pretty much anything that didn't require original lab or field research.

You were already a working writer when you went for an MFA. How come?

Pure ignorance. I didn't come from a family that went to school so had no idea how school worked or how teaching worked. I got an MFA because I looked at ads for teaching faculty and they often said that applicants need to have published "a book." I had a few! So if I got an MFA, I could go teach at a university and have an easy life.

I chose Western Connecticut State University because David Hartwell was on the board, so I figured it would be genre fiction friendly; because the program was low-residency, so no need to alter my life; and because the program insisted students write both creative work and practical work—so I'd just keep writing my usual fiction (creative) and articles/essays (practical) and get a degree for it. Well, once I got to my first residency, I read faculty member Kass Fleisher's memoir *Talking Out of School*, which is about her own struggles with academe. One line that jumped out at me was something like, "Nobody tells you that you can only teach at schools one tier below the one where you got your degree." Well, as a then-new state-run low-res MFA program, Westconn was the lowest, and nobody told me how it worked till I got there either!

So I teach at Westconn occasionally.

Ever try comix? Any luck with movies?
Yup! I wrote a couple small comics, and a graphic novel for VIZ when I worked there for *All You Need Is Kill*, which is the novel on which the film *Edge of Tomorrow* is based. There was also a manga adaptation of the novel, which blew my Western attempt out of the water. Whoops! I was also the English-language adapter of Junji Ito's *Frankenstein* manga, which won an Eisner Award.

My short novel *Under My Roof* was optioned by a director of TV commercials, and I wrote the first and third drafts of the script. When we were pitching the book itself around in the old days, one of the Big Five publishers said to my agent, "Instead of a nuclear bomb, couldn't the kid have a girlfriend?" By the sixth draft of the film script, written by the director's wife, the kid had a girlfriend. By the seventh draft, that girlfriend was gone. They even shot several minutes of the film, so the option was realized and I got a payout. But no more footage was shot, and the director stopped answering my emails years ago.

So, sure, I'm luckier than 99 percent of all the daydreamers out there, and 95 percent of all the writers! No movie though.

Most SF writers aspire to be a presenter at the Academy Awards someday. What are your chances?
Slim, but not none.

Around the turn of the century you wrote a number of articles for the Village Voice. *Do you ever get sentimental about New York?*
Yes, but only between visits. Giuliani and Bloomberg really ruined that town. Even the Bowery has been gentrified after three hundred years of resistance. I get sentimental about the 1990s, not about New York. Of course, now I live in the Bay Area, which is like a young adult novel dystopia. You're either a zillionaire with cosmic technological powers or a bad week away from being homeless.

You said it, Nick.

Ring, Ring, Ring, Ring, Ring, Ring, Ring

Author's note: I would like to thank Jeffrey Thomas for his invitation to write a story using the concepts, species, and technologies of his expansive and venerable "Punktown" setting.

IT WAS USUALLY DISMISSED as a kid's toy but Janice Steinberg still loved the Ouija phone, though she was pushing forty years old and it was obviously having some sort of net negative effect on her existence. Paxton's nightlife was a dangerous thing compared to even the wildest lawless interzones on Earth, but she could hang. Could have hanged, anyways, were she not home every night, tuning in, caressing the pulsing little wet-plastic brain nailed to the classic wooden board. Her Ouija phone was old school, with a heavy black receiver and a coiling snakelike cable attaching it to the medulla oblongata of that selfsame translucent plastic model of a human brain, the interior of which swirled with wisps of green light, each one decidedly not a spirit but just some goofy-cum-spooky gimmick the manufacturer thought would impress the rubes, and boy did it.

Janice thought she saw something in those gimmick lights anyway, something like multiple consciousnesses in how they flitted about like tiny fish whenever Janice made a call. She thought she heard sense-making too, through the handset though the dead mostly just talked to themselves and more rarely to one another. Scientists differed on what was going on, but ultimately they didn't care enough to study it, despite—because—the definitive answer to life after death was just a phone call away. Kids liked the Ouija phone because they could shout dirty words at their deceased grandparents, or at the poor lost Choom upon whose bones modern Paxton had been built. History loves a spoiled winner, after all, and Punktown loves a spoiled child. The Ouija phone was a nonsense machine, which is why the manufacturer never even released a model with a bell. Who was gonna call, anyway?

But enough backstory! One terrible night, Janice was alone in her room, the Ouija phone on her coffee table, mostly just lurking and occasionally attempting to intervene in what we may as well call "conversations." Ouija phones are party lines, when they want to be. Not all the voices are even human—anything with a soul would do, and we're not just speaking of the various humanoid races out in this big black universe of ours. Janice had once owned a spider monkey, and often wondered if she might come across its posthumous screeching one evening.

This night she heard a familiar howl and on a lark, called out to it: "Masashi, Masashi!" That had been the name of her monkey. And then a familiar voice called back, "Masashi?"

It wasn't the poor dead monkey, but it was a voice that made Janice squirm. She was wet. Her old lover, a male^2 Lubo named Tem. Janice had very much tried not to take it personally when Tem killed him^{2}self a decade prior, but it was still painful. Forget drugs, forget running out of Purple Vortex. Imagine being transported to a plane of existence where there was no such thing as Purple Vortex, where there had never been any such a thing as Purple Vortex, where even explaining the experience of consuming it was tantamount to a declaration of asylum-ready insanity.

That's what being fucked by a Lubo is like. Especially, the male^2 of the species.

"Masashi! I knew a human who owned a demihuman by that name!" said the voice of Tem through the Ouija phone.

For a long moment, Janice was silent. Tem had been nearly eight hundred years old when he finally ended him^{2}self. It wasn't her, he^2 had let her know. It was the universe, the centuries of drama and travail. Amazingly for a Lubo, he^2 had even developed a tiny pooch of belly flesh that marred his^2 otherwise perfect body of swirled marble. Tem wanted to go out with a trace of dignity. She missed him so much.

Finally, she shouted, a horrible yawp.

Tem cried out from amidst the din of a billion dead, "Janice! It is you!"

"Tem . . . Tem," she said. "You're . . ." She almost said *alive* but swallowed the word because it was insipid.

Then, "You're there."

"Janice," Tem said. "It's so . . . this plane of post-existence, you need to understand. Please pay close attention to what I am about to tell you." And he spoke at length about life after death, existence after Oasis, time after Punktown. Too soon, it was daylight. Janice knew what she must do.

Assault engines are expensive, but widely available if you knew the right people, and despite having spent the last decade fucking around mostly with a Ouija phone, Janice still knew a few people.

She had to take all her money out of the bank and make up the shortfall by getting on her knees and doing a little business with the Kilian gang that had an engine going spare. After a quick run-through of the assault engine's many capabilities, she inquired as to which Kilian religious sect the gang members belonged and made a mental note of it.

The bus ride was a long one, and Janice was the only passenger with an assault engine, which garnered her a few dirty looks from others as she took up two seats, and littered the floor with satchels full of various ammunition. She signaled to stop by a university district that housed a number of inexpensive restaurants, ramshackle housing, and a variety of places of worship catering to the large and multispecies student body. When Janice found the main temple of the minority sect that was the ideological competitor to her Kilian associates, she opened fire.

One might think that a relatively untrained woman wouldn't get very far in a mission of random, wanton destruction, given both the state of law enforcement in Paxton—ridiculously violent and fairly unsentimental—and the many unusual martial abilities of the neighborhood's various residents. But an assault engine is quite a piece of merchandise. Micromissiles bored into the load-bearing walls of the Kilian temple, vaporized the girders, and collapsed the building into its own footprint. From the rear, blue plasma capsules sprayed out in a conical formation, liquidating the forcers that had come roaring up the boulevard to put Janice down.

Janice screamed, "This is a rescue attempt!" and took out another building, this one a low pillbox from which the batoi-deac L'Lewed perform their sacred purification ritual of forcing themselves down the throats of primitive primates in order to be posthumously shat out, cleansed of karmic shame. Had poor lost Masashi the spider monkey, who foolishly ran away from Janice one evening six years ago, been among the sacrifices? That, friends, we still do not know.

Torgessi philosophy students voted to act and then moved to stampede over Janice, only to be brought down by a fusillade of black crystal bullets. The rounds couldn't penetrate thick Torgessi hides, but the shattered material immediately expanded into great whips of barbed obsidian, and that *did* pierce the eyes and other orifices of the students, leaving the beef-men multiply skewered on a block-long hedgerow of crystal thorns, which itself formed a handy barricade against other would-be defenders of the assorted *qōḏeš haqqŏḏāšīm* Janice was primed to destroy.

The solution was clearly to deploy more forcers, themselves outfitted with assault engines sufficient to vanquish Janice, but it was feared that the inevitable shootout would level too many houses of worship and scholarship, and the social repercussions would be felt for decades. A single Ramon awoke from her noontime meditations, scampered up to a nearby roof, and with self-confident *mreooww* flung herself at Janice, drawing her sword mid-multistory leap. All of Punktown gasped, hearts and other organs soaring, as the Ramon effortlessly curled into a front shoulder roll, blade sparking against cobblestone, and unfurled to strike, only to stagger, lose her grip on the hilt of her sword—which hit the ground and bounced, clanging—fall to her knees, then collapse and die at Janice's feet thanks to the invisible, undetectable-save-for-noting that-someone-just-died-at-Janice's-feet poison gas formulated exclusively for nonhuman nervous systems the assault engine had been pumping out since Janice first pulled one of the many, many triggers she had decided to try.

After that, it was clearly time to call in the big guns, *id est*, us, official representatives of Paxton Hologram & Virtual Technologies, *id est*, the telephone company. Our illustrious founders had buried something—well, some say *found* something—and then secured it in place with a painful and exploitive nanofiber lattice harness under a nearby street a century ago and it was best that grue and carnage presently sluicing into the sewers due to the actions of Janice Steinberg didn't whet its appetite for more. My associate Augustus, a talented and passionate member of the Kodju race, cut through the aether and caused us to materialize several feet over the head of and a few inches immediately behind Janice.

Our orders were to take her alive, unless we couldn't. We're the phone company, after all, not a pack of drug-addled assassins.

Augustus's long legs brought us to ground within a tenth-second of our entry onto the field of battle. I hopped out of Augustus's left ear and alighted onto the posterosuperior quadrant on Janice's skull, quickly found the vestibulocochlear nerve, gave it a venomous nibble, and leapt back to safety as she fell. Augustus reached over and snatched the bulky assault engine out of her hands with one of his platterlike paws.

Good work, Jeff, he subvocalized, which filled his ear canal, and I tapped my zillion tiny pseudopods upon his cavum concha, as if to say to him, *Aha, that poor dead cat! Good thing I don't have a nervous system at all and that you leave most of yours on your native plane of existence during working hours.*

Augustus surely would have enjoyed crushing Janice in his hands, shoving the resulting goo into his mouth and then letting it express through the gaps between his teeth to decorate his chins and chest, but of course the Kodju are all about bloody vengeance. I, a tiny Mee'hi, by way of contrast, am loath to take any more violent action than is strictly necessary to close an outstanding customer support or equipment repair ticket. It is thus through our dialectical opposition that my old mutt comrade Augustus and I achieve superior solutions for our team, H&VT, and all of Paxton. Augustus satisfied himself by raising the assault engine high over his head, and with a mighty flex of his muscles, kinking two of the three hot barrels unto total disrepair.

The forcers and cleanup crews will be here soon enough, Augustus hummed to himself. I tapped *Then, comrade, let us see what we can see about our customer before she is dragged away to some fell and distant dungeon.* I had enough of Janice Steinberg's DNA smeared on my mandibles to feed into the H&VT tablet Augustus carried for me, and from there all that the telephone company knew about her was revealed, and that was plenty.

Janice Steinberg was your typical "bananaphone" customer— multiplanar data plan, unlimited psychoactive inhalants, untranslatabledibles, *et aliae*. Yes, Steinberg was a woman, and thus so was her telephonic services profile. And oh-ho, what was this, a Ouija phone! With monthly overages! Augustus reverberated to me, *Forget waiting for the fuzz, let's bring her back to her home and do a hardware check.* I tapped out the many torts we'd be committing by doing such a thing, but it was just for show in case our team supervisor had the scene under surveillance. Augustus translated us all to the Steinberg residence, and plopped Janice, still unconscious but slowly awakening, onto her couch.

I slid down Augustus's arm and, with a patented flea-leap, alighted onto the Ouija phone. It was still wet, and warm, and frothy. I scuttled around the underside to check the wiring and sniff for shorts, as Augustus read off Janice's recent billed activity aloud in the utterly incomprehensible language of his people, which sounded quite a bit like several human beings purposefully shuffling across a wooden floor in stocking feet. I was too far away to call out to him to speak our common tongue, so made the gimmicked "fish" lights blink in code till he noticed and acquiesced.

"Lots of delivery calls to local restaurants. Usual peri-mastur-batory psychoactives for a human of her age and gender—ugh, why did I decide to sit in this particular chair, Jeff—and what appears to be the spoor of intense tribal affiliations."

TRIBALS? I made the lights blink.

"R. Steinberg, H. Steinberg, and the like," Augustus said. "At clearly ritual times as well. Every week ninety minutes with R., on fifth day. Much shorter communiqués with H, usually in the morn-ings. Perhaps her terror attack on the university district's religious centers had a sectarian motivation."

AH, FAMILY, I morsed. AND LIKELY NOT CLOSE EITHER, SINCE SHE IS CALLING THEM REGULARLY RATHER THAN TAKING VISI-TORS HERE OR ACCRUING ROAMING CHARGES BY TRAVELING TO SEE THEM.

Augustus roared with laughter. "Haha, family! I get it! Good one, Jeff!" The room shook, and Janice began to stir. I zipped over to the edge of the coffee table and hurled myself back into Augustus's ear to better interrogate our customer as to her telephonic needs and her murder spree.

Let me do the talking, old mutt, I tapped onto the surface of his cavum concha. *Try to enunciate and say what I say.* Augustus snorted his agreement and waved casually to Janice as her head jerked up from the couch cushions with a start.

"Hello, we are from the phone company," Augustus said, flashing his work ID card, and then gesturing to the tiny pixel on the corner of his card that represented my own identification number and portrait. "We believe you may have a malfunctioning Ouija phone."

Janice laughed the laugh of a newly christened murderess. "Oh no, Mister . . ."

"Augustus. And Jeff."

"Oh no, Mister Augustusnjeff," Janice said, "I may well have the only truly operational Ouija phone in existence. I communicated through it. With someone I once knew in life. He was called Tem, and he was a Lubo."

"Ah, so you were lovers," I told Augustus to say, and he did, and he did so without a giggle, which I appreciated.

"Why do you assume we were lovers? Just because he was a Lubo, and I a human being?"

"Yes, of course," we told her. "Plus, we do have access to your complete telephonic history. Lubo don't usually pick up the phone if the call is not from someone with which they are rutting. We know all about your monkey too. It made some calls. Bananaphone."

Janice held back some kind of cough. "Did you just say," she said, slowly, "'with which they are rutting'?"

"Fucking?" I tried. Some human idiomatic expressions are lost on me. "Love-making-with!" I had Augustus yelp out, a little too quickly. Janice snorted at that one, then sighed.

"Well, you're right, I guess. It is all impossible to describe, what we do with one another in the dark, isn't it?" she said. "I'm just protective of my memories of him is all."

"You killed several dozen people today," I reminded her through Augustus.

"It was a rescue operation." She glanced over at the Ouija phone, hungrily. Or so Augustus told me later, as from my vantage point in his ear I could not see her expression, and honestly even if I could I doubt I would have decided she was hungry for her phone. Maybe *lustily* so, but explain that to Augustus for me yourself!

"Tem spoke to me at length about the dimension in which he now liv—uh, resides. Do you have religious beliefs, Mister Augustusnjeff?" Janice asked, sounding a bit like a murderer.

Well, just answer her, I tapped at him, and Augustus launched into an extensive exegesis on Kodju spirituality, which had much to do with suffering and nature and swirling infinities and an omnipresent matrix of dynamic duality which limned all of existence and suchlike flummery. I took the opportunity to crawl out of his ear and down his spine, then trudge across the carpet, snake up the far leg of the coffee table, and reenter the guts of the phone. Augustus was on his feet now, gesturing broadly and tracing some diagram of the universe and cycles of metempsychosis that conveniently placed Kodju several rungs higher than *Homo sapiens sapiens* on the great ladder of inculpation while Janice tried to get a word in edgewise.

"Have you ever considered the possibility that you may be insane?" she blurted out.

"Have you?" Augustus countered. "You're the one who thinks you're actually having conversations via Ouija phone."

"Doesn't H&VT manufacture and sell them precisely for that purpose?" Janice said.

"We only license the technology," Augustus said. "Huma'am, I have mastered the discipline of interplanar travel. Let me assure you that my people know what awaits—"

"You know nothing!" Janice shouted. "Tem knows! I know. And what awaits us is—" and she pronounced some words that sent Augustus reeling. He flailed, his knuckles grazing the ceiling, and he staggered backward onto Janice's masturbation chair, which collapsed under him.

"No, no! Impossible! The sages of Kjodyor say . . ."

"Lies!" Janice said, and then she repeated the philosophical terms with which she had laid Augustus low. He was a strong fellow, resolute in his faith and a quality worker, but I almost began to worry for him. He cleverly clamped his giant mitts over his ears and avoided Janice's next theologico-rhetorical assault, but he, I suspect, could read her lips, and his own face was twisted up in an anguish I rarely see in bipedal organisms.

If, reader, you are curious as to why I was not negatively affected by what Janice Steinberg declared to be The Unbelievable Truth of It All as Handed Up from Down Low by the beautiful Lubo male[2] yclept Tem, it is for three reasons—first, the Mee'hi have no religion as we are far too intelligent for such things, and two, all Mee'hi live in nests made from the heads of beings much larger than ourselves.

We swarm them, be they biped or quadruped, poison them, kill them, rend their flesh from the neck or necks down and sell it to the gourmands of various other species, and live out our days in anarcho-communist bliss among the rotting but still delicious neuralfruits of a sapionoid brainpan. To put it more simply, we've not only heard all this stuff before—we eat it, then we poop it back out, then we fuck atop it, lay our eggs into it, then hatch out of it and do it all over again, and every few weeks. Stick with the Mee'hi, chums, we know what's what.

The third reason was that I was only half-listening because I was busy diagnosing the phone. It had gone bad—brain rot caused by a radiation leak due to consumer mishandling. I filled out a scent-form to bring back to the office and waited for my chance to end this game.

My hope and stratagem was that the inevitable loggerheads caused by religious argument would compel Janice to try to prove her point by snatching up the handset of the Ouija phone and calling for her poor lost Tem, or perhaps even poor lost Masashi, to provide corroborating testimony. Augustus uncovered his ears to hear Janice's justification for her actions. Ouija phones can work, provided love is true and luck in the air, she explained. The souls of the dead are being held captive and must be rescued by those currently living, on this plane, after their own deaths. Thus, the most devout members of communities of faith needed to be transported en masse to the holding cell, so that the spoiled children of Paxton could hear their cries for help and thus shrug off their childish ways and grow up with a spirit of collective dread and solidarity that would impel them to form an army of posthumous liberation so to overthrow the regime of the dead which so bedeviled, beraped, and inconvenienced her former lover. Thus freed, Tem would proceed to run for high office in the Republic of the Damned, and Janice would sit at, or on, his right hand after she died of the brain cancer Tem told her she had gotten from overexposure to Ouija phone radiation.

"Tem, Tem, are you there! Can you hear me?" she called into the handset as she beckoned Augustus to crawl over and listen in, and just as I crawled into the handset and took up a position in the transmitter. "It's me, Janice! I did what you said I should do. Have the new friends arrived yet?"

"Uh . . . yes, hello hello, it is I, Tem," I said. "We're rolling out the rugs and hanging out the sheets to dry down here for all your poor unfortunate victims. It's all real swell, Ms. Steinberg. You did a great humanlike job with your task this morning. Everything is hunky-dory!"

It is not as though I believed I could deceive Janice Steinberg even for a moment. I had simply needed the time to examine the phone, to make sure its malfunction wasn't due to manufacturer error, or a software problem, though I admit I did kick myself when I called her "Ms. Steinberg"—surely Tem had had a diminutive nickname for his human rutfriend, like "Steiny" or "Jay Cee" or something.

Through no fault of Paxton Hologram & Virtual Technologies or its licensees, the sick brain of the malfunctioning Ouija phone had transmitted its disease to the living mind of Janice Steinberg, and that disease sparked the day's bloody events. My only option now was to pronounce the preselected mission-specific safe word *hunky-dory* loudly enough for Augustus to hear, which my position in the handset transmitter allowed. He fell into a hypnotic state and translated his mass to another plane of existence through a circuitous route that momentarily exposed the contents of Janice Steinberg's living room to temperature only slightly over the 2.7 Kelvin of deep space. So that killed her off—contra our mission parameters, but for the greater good of our user base—and flash froze everything in the room, including me for a nonce.

Upon my return to consciousness, I had naught to do but rewire the Ouija phone to make an outgoing cellular call so that I could get a pickup. Augustus would be traveling transdimensionally and unconsciously until it was time to report for our next shift, as a safety precaution. I surely was not going to flea-jump all the way back to the office after today's exhausting job, and it is extremely difficult for Mee'hi to hail a cab in Punktown. No pockets, you see.

I make a note that I spent a significant amount of time in this most unusual and damaged—through no fault of Paxton Hologram & Virtual Technologies—Ouija phone for a reason. As I mentioned when I began spinning this yarn, friend, Ouija phones are nonsense devices. The consumer hears what she wishes to hear, and given the truth of it all, most consumers actually do wish to hear nonsense and nothing but, and they wish to hear it on their own terms. That's why there's no bell. Who's gonna call? Nobody you want to hear from.

Which is why, as I waited for my pick up by eating some of the defrosted strands of Janice Steinberg's dark and curly hair, thinking of what a lovely Mee'hi warren her skull would make, I nearly jumped right out of my exoskeleton when the Ouija phone on the coffee table, still glowing green with swirling green light, with the handset still off the hook, and with my jury-rigged rewire to catch a totally quotidian cellular signal, began to ring. And I knew the call was for me, but I dared not crawl up into the receiver and listen to the message.

And you, child! If your wet-plastic brained Ouija phone ever rings, my sweet friend, please leave the handset on the hook, please please avert your eyes from the swirling green lights within the translucent braincase, and please please please call your local H&VT office via some other form of telephony.

Bibliography

Fiction Books

The Second Shooter. Solaris Books, forthcoming.

The Planetbreaker's Son. PM Press, 2021.

Sabbath. Tor Books, 2019.

The People's Republic of Everything (short story collection). Tachyon Publications, 2018.

I Am Providence. Skyhorse Publishing, 2016. (In Turkish as *Lovecraft'in Külleri.* Nemesis Kitap, 2017.)

The Nickronomicon (short story collection). Innsmouth Free Press, 2014.

The Last Weekend. PS Publishing, 2014.

Love Is the Law. Dark Horse Books, 2013.

Bullettime. CZP, 2012.

The Damned Highway. (coauthor with Brian Keene). Dark Horse Books, 2011; Thunderstorm Books (limited/lettered) 2014.

Sensation. PM Press, 2011.

You Might Sleep . . . (short story collection). Prime Books, 2009.

Under My Roof. Soft Skull Press, 2007. (In German as *Unter meinem Dach.* Edition Phantasia, 2007; in Italian as *Come mio padre ha dichiarato guerra all'America.* Cargo, 2008.)

Move Under Ground: A Novel. Night Shade Books, 2004; Prime Books, 2006; and Dover Publications, 2020. (In German as *Abwärts: Move Under Ground.* Edition Phantasia, 2005; in Greek as *Pogia Kinesi.* Gemma Press, 2011.)

3000 MPH in Every Direction at Once: Stories and Essays. Prime Books, 2003.

Northern Gothic: A Novella. Soft Skull Press, 2001. (In German as *Northern Gothic: Eine New Yorker Schauergeschichte.* Edition Phantasia, 2007.)

Fiction Anthologies Edited or Coedited

Wonder and Glory Forever: Awe-Inspiring Lovecraftian Fiction. Dover Publications, 2020.

Mixed Up: Cocktail Recipes (And Flash Fiction) for the Discerning Drinker (and Reader) (coeditor with Molly Tanzer). Skyhorse, 2017.

Saiensu Fikushon (coeditor with Masumi Washington). VIZ Media, 2016.

Hanzai Japan (coeditor with Masumu Washington). VIZ Media, 2015.

Phantasm Japan (coeditor with Masumi Washington). VIZ Media, 2014.

The Future Is Japanese (coeditor with Masumi Washington). VIZ Media, 2012.

Haunted Legends (coeditor with Ellen Datlow). Tor Books, 2010.

Realms 2 (coeditor with Sean Wallace). Wyrm Publishing, 2009.

Spicy Slipstream Stories (coeditor with Jay Lake). Lethe Books, 2008.

Realms (coeditor with Sean Wallace). Wyrm Publishing, 2008.

The Urban Bizarre. Prime Books, 2004.

Nonfiction Books

The Battle Royale Slam Book (coeditor with Masumi Washington). VIZ Media, 2014.

Quotes Every Man Should Know. Quirk Books, 2013.

Insults Every Man Should Know. Quirk Books, 2011.

Starve Better: Surviving the Endless Horror of the Writing Life. Apex Publications, 2011.

Peer-Reviewed Publications

Jai-eui Lee, *Kwangju Diary: Beyond Death, Beyond the Darkness of the Age* (coeditor and translator with Kap Su Seol). Los Angeles: UCLA Asian Pacific Monograph Series, 1999. (Also as *Gwangju Diary*. 518 Foundation, 2018.)

Poetry

Cthulhu Senryu (chapbook). Wildside Press, 2006.

For a more complete bibliography including stories, articles, essays, and more, visit http://www.nick-mamatas.com/bibliography.php.

About the Author

NICK MAMATAS IS THE author of several novels, including *I Am Providence*, *Sabbath*, and the forthcoming *The Second Shooter*. His short fiction has appeared in *Best American Mystery Stories*, *Year's Best Science Fiction & Fantasy*, and many other venues; the best of the last decade was recently collected in *The People's Republic of Everything*. Nick is also an editor and anthologist: his forthcoming title *Wonder and Glory Forever* collects classic and recent awe-inspiring Lovecraftian fiction. Nick's fiction and editorial work has won a Bram Stoker Award, and been nominated for the Hugo, World Fantasy, Locus, and Shirley Jackson awards.

FRIENDS OF
PM

These are indisputably momentous times—the financial system is melting down globally and the Empire is stumbling. Now more than ever there is a vital need for radical ideas.

In the years since its founding—and on a mere shoestring—PM Press has risen to the formidable challenge of publishing and distributing knowledge and entertainment for the struggles ahead. With hundreds of releases to date, we have published an impressive and stimulating array of literature, art, music, politics, and culture. Using every available medium, we've succeeded in connecting those hungry for ideas and information to those putting them into practice.

Friends of PM allows you to directly help impact, amplify, and revitalize the discourse and actions of radical writers, filmmakers, and artists. It provides us with a stable foundation from which we can build upon our early successes and provides a much-needed subsidy for the materials that can't necessarily pay their own way. You can help make that happen—and receive every new title automatically delivered to your door once a month—by joining as a Friend of PM Press. And, we'll throw in a free T-shirt when you sign up.

Here are your options:

- $30 a month: Get all books and pamphlets plus 50% discount on all webstore purchases
- $40 a month: Get all PM Press releases (including CDs and DVDs) plus 50% discount on all webstore purchases
- $100 a month: Superstar—Everything plus PM merchandise, free downloads, and 50% discount on all webstore purchases

For those who can't afford $30 or more a month, we have Sustainer Rates at $15, $10, and $5. Sustainers get a free PM Press T-shirt and a 50% discount on all purchases from our website.

Your Visa or Mastercard will be billed once a month, until you tell us to stop. Or until our efforts succeed in bringing the revolution around. Or the financial meltdown of Capital makes plastic redundant. Whichever comes first.

PM Press is an independent, radical publisher of books and media to educate, entertain, and inspire. Founded in 2007 by a small group of people with decades of publishing, media, and organizing experience, PM Press amplifies the voices of radical authors, artists, and activists. Our aim is to deliver bold political ideas and vital stories to all walks of life and arm the dreamers to demand the impossible. We have sold millions of copies of our books, most often one at a time, face to face. We're old enough to know what we're doing and young enough to know what's at stake. Join us to create a better world.

PM Press
PO Box 23912
Oakland, CA 94623
510-658-3906 • info@pmpress.org

PM Press in Europe
europe@pmpress.org
www.pmpress.org.uk

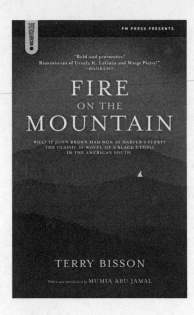

Fire on the Mountain

**Terry Bisson with an Introduction
by Mumia Abu-Jamal**
$15.95
ISBN: 978-1-60486-087-0
5 by 8 • 208 pages

It's 1959 in socialist Virginia. The Deep
South is an independent Black nation
called Nova Africa. The second Mars
expedition is about to touch down on
the red planet. And a pregnant scientist
is climbing the Blue Ridge in search of
her great-great grandfather, a teenage
slave who fought with John Brown
and Harriet Tubman's guerrilla army.

Long unavailable in the U.S., published in France as *Nova Africa*, *Fire on the
Mountain* is the story of what might have happened if John Brown's raid on
Harper's Ferry had succeeded—and the Civil War had been started not by
the slave owners but the abolitionists.

> *"History revisioned, turned inside out ... Bisson's
> wild and wonderful imagination has taken some
> strange turns to arrive at such a destination."*
> —Madison Smartt Bell, Anisfield-Wolf Award
> winner and author of Devil's Dream

Judenstaat

Simone Zelitch
$20.00
ISBN: 978-1-62963-713-6
6 by 9 • 336 pages

It is 1988. Judit Klemmer is a film-maker who is assembling a fortieth-anniversary official documentary about the birth of Judenstaat, the Jewish homeland surrendered by defeated Germany in 1948. Her work is complicated by Cold War tensions between the competing U.S. and Soviet empires and by internal conflicts among the "black-hat" Orthodox Jews, the far more worldly Bundists, and reactionary Saxon nationalists who are still bent on destroying the new Jewish state.

But Judit's work has far more personal complications. A widow, she has yet to deal with her own heart's terrible loss—the very public assassination of her husband, Hans Klemmer, shot dead while conducting a concert.

Then a shadowy figure slips her a note with new and potentially dangerous information about her famous husband's murder.

> "Judenstaat *uses the technique of alternate history to offer biting commentary on modern Israel, on the post–Cold War era in which we live, and on religion and nationhood.*"
> —Cory Doctorow, coeditor of Boing Boing
> and author of Little Brother

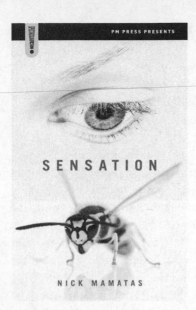

PM PRESS PRESENTS

Sensation

Nick Mamatas
$14.95
ISBN: 978-1-60486-354-3
5 by 8 • 208 pages

Love. Politics. Parasitic manipulation. Julia Hernandez left her husband, shot a real-estate developer out to gentrify Brooklyn, and then vanished without a trace. Well, perhaps one or two traces were left . . . With different personal and consumption habits, Julia has slipped out of the world she knew and into the Simulacrum—a place between the cracks of our existence from which human history is both guided and thwarted by the conflict between a species of anarchist wasp and a collective of hyperintelligent spiders. When Julia's ex-husband Raymond spots her in a grocery store he doesn't usually patronize, he's drawn into an underworld of radical political gestures and Internet organizing looking to overthrow a ruling class it knows nothing about—and Julia is the new media sensation of both this world and the Simulacrum.

Told ultimately from the collective point of view of another species, *Sensation* plays with the elements of the Simulacrum we all already live in: media reports, businessspeak, blog entries, text messages, psychological evaluation forms, and the always fraught and kindly lies lovers tell one another.

> *"Nick Mamatas' brilliant comic novel,* Sensation, *reads*
> *like an incantation that both vilifies and celebrates*
> *the complex absurdity of the modern world."*
> —*Lucius Shepard, winner of the Hugo,*
> *Nebula, and World Fantasy awards*